"If I don't let you go now, we'll end up in my bedroom."

"Maybe it's time we gave in to this. Maybe it's time we grab what we can now. Before it's too late."

"You're not the type of woman who has an affair."

"No, I'm not. At least, not with just any man. But with you… I want to feel you again, Adam. I want to touch your skin and let you touch mine."

"Leigh."

His voice was a sharp warning, and she knew her words were as arousing as anything else they might do. Somehow she managed, "I've missed you, Adam." It had taken her this long to realize the emptiness inside of her had always been her loss of Adam. No other man had come close to filling up that space.

"If I touch you—" His hand stopped in midair.

"Touch me," she whispered.

But instead of touching her, he kissed her.

Now there was no turning back.

Dear Reader,

Well, if it's true that March comes in like a lion and goes out like a lamb, you're going to need some fabulous romantic reads to get you through the remaining cold winter nights. Might we suggest starting with a new miniseries by bestselling author Sherryl Woods? In *Isn't It Rich?*, the first of three books in Ms. Wood's new MILLION DOLLAR DESTINIES series, we meet Richard Carlton, one of three brothers given untold wealth from his aunt Destiny. But in pushing him toward beautiful—if klutzy—PR executive Melanie Hart, Aunt Destiny provides him with riches that even money can't buy!

In *Bluegrass Baby* by Judy Duarte, the next installment in our MERLYN COUNTY MIDWIVES miniseries, a handsome but commitment-shy pediatrician shares a night of passion with a down-to-earth midwife. But what will he do when he learns there might be a baby on the way? Karen Rose Smith continues the LOGAN'S LEGACY miniseries with *Take a Chance on Me*, in which a sexy, single CEO finds the twin sister he never knew he had—and in the process is reunited with the only woman he ever loved. In *Where You Least Expect It* by Tori Carrington, a fugitive accused of a crime he didn't commit decides to put down roots and dare to dream of the love, life and family he thought he'd never have. Arlene James wraps up her miniseries THE RICHEST GALS IN TEXAS with *Tycoon Meets Texan!* in which a handsome billionaire who can have any woman he wants sets his sights on a beautiful Texas heiress. She clearly doesn't need his money, so *whatever* can she want with him? And when a police officer opens his door to a nine-months-pregnant stranger in the middle of a blizzard, he finds himself called on to provide both personal and professional services, in *Detective Daddy* by Jane Toombs.

So bundle up, and take heart—spring is coming! And so are six more sensational stories about love, life and family, coming next month from Silhouette Special Edition!

All the best,

Gail Chasan
Senior Editor

Take a Chance on Me

KAREN ROSE SMITH

Silhouette®
SPECIAL EDITION®
Published by Silhouette Books
America's Publisher of Contemporary Romance

Special thanks and acknowledgment are given
to Karen Rose Smith for her contribution
to the LOGAN'S LEGACY series.

To Edie, my critique partner, my phone sister, my second set of eyes.
I'm so grateful we're friends.

With deep appreciation to my research sources: My Portland contacts—
Doreen Roberts and Leah Vale; my transplant experts—
Dr. Danil Hammoudi, Dr. Meir Wetzler; as well as Linda Goodnight and her son
Dr. Travis Goodnight. Thanks also to Judy Duarte and Lynda Sandoval,
who made coordination of the prequel books easy.

SILHOUETTE BOOKS

ISBN 0-373-24599-8

TAKE A CHANCE ON ME

This edition published by arrangement with Harlequin Books S.A.

Visit Silhouette at www.eHarlequin.com

Printed in U.S.A.

Books by Karen Rose Smith

Silhouette Special Edition

Abigail and Mistletoe #930
The Sheriff's Proposal #1074
His Little Girl's Laughter #1426
Expecting the CEO's Baby #1535
Their Baby Bond #1588
Take a Chance on Me #1599

Silhouette Books

The Fortunes of Texas
Marry in Haste...

Silhouette Romance

**Adam's Vow* #1075
**Always Daddy* #1102
**Shane's Bride* #1128
†*Cowboy at the Wedding* #1171
†*Most Eligible Dad* #1174
†*A Groom and a Promise* #1181
The Dad Who Saved Christmas #1267
‡*Wealth, Power and a Proper Wife* #1320
‡ *Love, Honor and a Pregnant Bride* #1326
‡*Promises, Pumpkins and Prince Charming* #1332
The Night Before Baby #1348
‡*Wishes, Waltzes and a Storybook Wedding* #1407
Just the Man She Needed #1434
Just the Husband She Chose #1455
Her Honor-Bound Lawman #1480
Be My Bride? #1492
Tall, Dark & True #1506
Her Tycoon Boss #1523
Doctor in Demand #1536
A Husband in Her Eyes #1577
The Marriage Clause #1591
Searching for Her Prince #1612
With One Touch #1638
The Most Eligible Doctor #1692

*Darling Daddies
†The Best Men
‡ Do You Take This Stranger?

Previously published under the pseudonym Kari Sutherland

Silhouette Special Edition

Wish on the Moon #741

Silhouette Romance

Heartfire, Homefire #973

KAREN ROSE SMITH

Award-winning author Karen Rose Smith first glimpsed the Southwest on a cross-country train ride when she was sixteen. Although she has lived in Pennsylvania all her life, New Mexico has always called to her. The mountains there have a power and beauty she hopes she managed to convey in this book. Readers can reach Karen at her Web site (www.karenrosesmith.com) or write to her at P.O. Box 1545, Hanover, PA 17331.

THE PORTLAND PRESS

Rare Blood Disorder Reunites Twins Separated As Infants!

Portland, OR, March 2004—Adam Bartlett, sexy, single CEO of Novel Programs, Unlimited, was reunited with twin sister Lissa Cartwright Grayson—the woman who snagged her *own* most eligible bachelor last month—after their biological father tracked Adam down in the hopes of saving his younger son's life. Sources tell the *Press* that eight-year-old Mark Cambry collapsed during a soccer game and was diagnosed with a rare blood disorder last year. Witnesses called the reunion between the twins "heartwarming" and "beautiful." Adam Bartlett's business partner, Dylan Montgomery, had this to say, "Adam's reaction at learning he had a sibling—let alone a *twin*—was nothing short of pleased shock." Word also has it that the moment he arrived at Portland General to start the proceedings, Adam had another unexpected reunion—with his long-ago love, Nurse Leigh Peters. Is it possible that before the month is out, Adam will go from bachelor businessman to heroic husband?

Chapter One

CEO Adam Bartlett rose to his feet.

The men and women sitting around the large mahogany table went silent, though Adam's former college roommate and present partner, Dylan Montgomery, winked at him. Adam almost smiled. At twenty-seven, he and Dylan ran the software firm they'd started after college. Who could have guessed they'd be this successful...this rich...this respected?

Towering above his board of directors, Adam glanced down at the papers on the table before him. He didn't actually need notes. ''Good morning, everyone. I called this meeting to discuss the success of our latest product line. Our recent endeavors have produced another winner. Since most companies who have networks have jumped on the bandwagon—''

Unexpectedly, the door to the conference room swung open. His pretty brunette receptionist, Darlene, looked harried. Though she'd only been with Novel Programs, Unlimited, for a few months, she knew better than to interrupt his board meetings.

Now, however, she waved her hand toward his office suite down the hall. "I'm terribly sorry to interrupt you, Mr. Bartlett, but there's a man out here who demanded he be shown to your office. He won't take no for an answer. He insists this is a matter of life and death."

Over the years, through his company's meteoric rise, Adam had managed to stay out of the limelight and away from the public. "What's his name?"

"Jared Cambry."

The name wasn't familiar unless Adam had met the man at a conference or a merger meeting. He looked over at Dylan, but Dylan shook his head indicating he didn't recognize the name, either.

"He said he's a lawyer," Darlene added in a rush as if in her agitation she'd forgotten that important detail.

Adam pushed his hand through his thick brown hair, accepting the fact his day was going to take a sharp left turn onto a road he didn't expect. To the board, he said, "Dylan will take over the meeting and keep me posted on everything you discuss. Hopefully I'll be back in a few minutes."

As sandy-haired Dylan took Adam's place at the head of the table, Adam exited the room and started down the hall to his office. The door was ajar, and

Adam spotted a man around his own six-two height pacing the room.

"Jared Cambry?" Adam asked, examining the man's features, his dark-brown hair, thinking something about him seemed familiar. Though the lawyer appeared to be in his midforties, if the tension lines on his forehead persisted, he would age fast.

Cambry stared at Adam for a long moment. "Are you Adam Bartlett?"

"Yes. I only have a few minutes. I'm in the middle of a board meeting."

"This could take more than a few minutes," Cambry said wearily. "Can we sit down?"

"Mr. Cambry, I have a tight schedule today. If you'd like to make an appointment for later in the week—"

"This can't wait. I need to talk to you now. My son is dying." He stopped abruptly, then took a moment to compose himself.

Adam took a few steps deeper into the office, closer to Cambry. "I'm sorry about that, but I don't understand what it has to do with me."

When Cambry squared his shoulders, his expression became unreadable. "I'm your father."

Everything inside of Adam went still. His adoptive mother had only told him his mother's name had been Olivia and she'd been a teenager when he was born. When Adam had searched for further information after he'd turned eighteen, he'd discovered that a fire and power outage at Portland General and The Children's Connection Adoption Center had wiped out hard drives that had stored confidential as well as necessary information.

Adam's childhood with his adoptive family had not been a happy one. How he'd longed to find and know his real parents....

Hope nudged a frozen part of his heart open, but before he could ask any one of the myriad questions clicking through his head, before he could rejoice in the fact that he did indeed have a real father, Jared Cambry told Adam why he'd come.

"My son Mark has a rare blood disorder and needs a bone marrow transplant. His sister and brother aren't a match. Your sister, Lissa, isn't a match."

"My sister?"

This time, obviously not caring whether or not Adam sat, Cambry sank down into the wine leather chair in front of Adam's desk. "When I went searching for Olivia and her baby—" He stopped. "Maybe I should start at the beginning."

Automatically Adam closed the door to his office, feeling as if his whole world had suddenly tilted. He wouldn't be getting back to that board meeting, not until he learned every detail he possibly could about his background from Jared Cambry.

Unbuttoning his suit jacket, he sat on the corner of his desk and waited.

Cambry cut a look toward Adam, another out of the office building's window, then his gaze came back to rest on Adam again. "To put it simply, I got a girl pregnant in high school. Her name was Olivia Maddison. When she told me she was pregnant, I—"

Shifting uncomfortably, he cleared his throat. "I

came from a wealthy family, had plenty of money and offered it to her for an abortion. She wanted to have the baby. Then she told me to get out of her life because she intended to do without me or my money. After my family and I moved to Arizona, where I attended college, I contacted her, but she hung up on me. Around the baby's due date, I tried to call again, but her phone had been disconnected and I couldn't locate her."

When he looked away this time, Adam wondered what kind of man Jared Cambry was now. Did he still run from responsibility?

"Go on," Adam prompted, needing to know the whole story.

"I didn't get married until I was twenty-seven. Danielle and I had two kids, a boy and a girl, who came along eighteen months apart. Eight years after that, Danielle suddenly found herself pregnant again. That's when we had Mark."

Adam could see how Jared's face lit up at the thought of his younger son.

"Mark was sunshine from the minute he was born, always had a smile on his face, got along with everybody. I'm not sure why—maybe because of my roots and my past—I felt drawn back to Portland about a year ago, moved my family and opened a law office here. We were building a new life...a great life. Mark liked T-ball and soccer and we gave him hockey equipment for his eighth birthday. But then one day, he passed out while he was playing soccer, and we rushed him to the hospital. We learned he had this rare blood disease and without a bone marrow transplant, he won't make it past the age of ten."

Jared stopped, then pulled himself together again and went on. "Danielle and I were tested. So were Mark's sister and brother. None of us was a match. I couldn't sleep, couldn't concentrate on anything and then I remembered Olivia...and our baby."

Adam couldn't imagine any man forgetting that he had a child out in the world somewhere.

"I'd never told Danielle anything about her, but now Mark's life depended on finding Olivia. Danielle agreed we had to do everything possible so I hired a private investigator. Searching newspapers, he found that Olivia and her mother had been in an accident and taken to Portland General Hospital. From obits, he found that Mrs. Maddison died immediately after the accident and Olivia passed on a few weeks later."

Adam was beginning to get the gist of the search. "Your investigator went to Portland General?"

"Yes. But the hospital had suffered a fire and power outage that affected not only Portland General but The Children's Connection Clinic attached to it. Most records from that time had been destroyed. We got a break when we found out The Children's Connection personnel in recent years had taken time to input information from burned paper files and now they *did* have some sketchy information. We got bits and pieces—Olivia's name and a partial list of expenses sent to the state."

When Cambry rubbed his fingers back and forth across his temple, Adam could see this situation was hard on the man.

An instant later, Cambry continued, ''We couldn't tell exactly what info matched up. I had what I'd thought was your name—Adam Bartlite—but the address listed Valencia Vineyard about two hours outside of Portland. When I went there, I found Lissa who had been adopted by the Cartwrights. It turned out her birthday was the same one I had for you. With the obvious resemblance, you must be twins. Olivia was a twin—her sister died at birth.''

Not only a sister, but a twin. Adam tried to absorb that while he listened.

''Lissa was tested, but she's not a match, either. We finally discovered your last name had been misspelled on the records. My private investigator tracked you down. And here I am.''

''Does Lissa still live at the vineyard?''

''She does, and she's interested in meeting you. But she's away on her honeymoon right now.'' He glanced out the window again, then back at Adam. ''I know the chief of staff at the hospital. We can have your testing done today if you agree. We'll know in a week to ten days if you're a match.''

Trying to digest all of it piece by piece, Adam kept the impact of the news deep inside. He was used to not showing his feelings. He was used to not sharing what he was thinking about anything but business.

That's just the way it was.

He hated the idea of going back to the hospital where his adopted sister had died twenty years ago—the same hospital where doctors gave impersonal care to patients they didn't think twice about. He avoided memories of that day whenever he could. Over the years he'd learned to eat right and exercise so he didn't have to see doctors. Yet that could all change now if he agreed to do this.

Bringing out a handkerchief, Jared Cambry wiped his brow. He was sweating, and Adam understood why. "Did you say Mark is eight?"

"Yes. He's at home right now. But if you're a match and you agree to donate your bone marrow, he'll have to be admitted to the hospital to be prepped and have chemo and possibly radiation before the transplant."

Adam had been seven the day that the horse he loved had trampled his sister, the day his adoptive father had had the horse put down and Delia had died. At that age it had been close to impossible to understand life and death as well as hospital protocol. How could Cambry's young son deal with the idea of a bone marrow transplant or face the possibility of dying?

No matter what Jared Cambry had done or not done in the past, Adam couldn't know he had a half brother out there and *not* help him.

Looking Jared square in the eye, he decided, "Set up the testing and let's see if I'm a match."

When Christopher Chambers, Chief of Staff of Portland General Hospital, called Leigh Peters to his office, he told her, "I chose you because I knew you could handle this job of liaison well. You're one of the best pediatric oncology nurses I have, and I need you to smooth the waters for Jared Cambry."

Chambers was in his late fifties—tall, lean and gray-haired. Now he moved closer to the window and motioned to the hospital and annexes that made up Portland General's complex. "Jared is a large contributor to Portland General and we want to help him as best we can. As I told you, his son's full siblings aren't a match and neither was Lissa Cartwright. Now he has hope again with another half sibling. I want you to handle everyone concerned with kid gloves to make the process flow as easily as possible for them. Our lab's on alert to expedite matters as it did with Lissa Cartwright. Since you've dealt with Jared, his family and his son Mark on the boy's previous hospitalization, you already have a rapport with them."

"I understand, Dr. Chambers." Leigh loved her work as an oncology nurse in pediatrics. Although her aspirations would lead her to med school in June, a dream her mother had instilled before she was out of diapers, Leigh enjoyed working with people, too. She felt honored that Dr. Chambers had singled her out to help with this family.

"The donor will be here in a few minutes. The transplant counselor will meet with him after today's battery of tests. I want you to be his contact person. If at any time you need my input or authorization, call me, Leigh. Understand?"

She understood. She was supposed to grease the wheel and make sure Jared Cambry's road wasn't any harder than it had to be.

The chief of staff added, "I also want you to have someplace quiet where you can meet with Mark's potential donor. The conference room next to my office is vacant." He pulled a key from his pocket. "The file is already on the table there waiting for you. I don't want Mr. Bartlett to have to wait.''

''Bartlett?'' That name took Leigh back ten years. Certainly there had to be lots of Bartletts in the Portland area. Certainly it was no connection to Adam Bartlett, the young man she'd left ten years ago so she could have a future that was much better than her mother's.

''I have a meeting out of the hospital now.'' Chambers gave her a business card. ''But here's my cell phone number. Don't hesitate to use it if Bartlett has any questions you can't answer.''

Then Chambers walked to the elevator, and Leigh made her way to the conference room next door.

Purposely she turned her thoughts away from the past and what she'd left behind, to her future at Case Western University in Cleveland. Orientation started June fifth. She really should be more excited. Her lifetime goal was within her grasp. But she loved her work here and—

She opened the conference room door with her key and saw the file sitting on the conference table. She'd like to go through it thoroughly before Mr. Bartlett arrived. Leaving the door open, she crossed to the table, pulled out the chair and sat down to look at the file.

Her heart stopped. The name on the manilla folder was Adam Bartlett.

She'd no sooner flipped open the file than she heard footsteps in the corridor. Moments later, a tall, broad-shouldered man stepped inside.

Not just any man...Adam.

He froze when he saw her. His already serious face looked as if it had been carved from stone. ''Leigh?'' he asked as if he couldn't believe his eyes.

As she stood, his gaze passed over her quickly but thoroughly—her blond hair tied back in a ponytail because it was more sedate and professional-looking that way, her blue pantsuit, her uniform in Pediatric Oncology. She often wore smocks when caring for the kids, smocks that danced with animals or Disney characters or were tie-dyed to bring more color into the ward, but she'd left all those in her locker for this meeting.

''Hi, Adam.'' Flustered, she motioned to the table. ''I just got your file. I didn't realize who I'd be meeting today. You're Jared Cambry's son?''

After a moment's hesitation, Adam shrugged. ''Cambry insists that's what The Children's Connection Clinic's records say. Apparently he had a private investigator looking for me. He just found me this morning.''

That surprised her. Jared must have really pulled strings to get Adam's testing done today.

As the two of them stared at each other, Leigh easily recognized the boy Adam had been and realized she was even more attracted to the man he had become. His hair had been longer in high school. Today it was crisply cut in a no-nonsense businessman's style. His shoulders were broader now and filled out the expensive material of his suit jacket. The tie was Armani, the trousers perfectly creased. His Italian leather loafers were so different from the worn-out sneakers he'd sported as a teenager. His whole demeanor shouted success, and a hundred questions danced on her tongue. But they weren't here to discuss old times or to play catch up. Yet, she remembered how she'd left him....

His eyes, still so deeply green, had always mesmerized her. Reluctantly she broke eye contact and motioned to the table. "I haven't had a chance to look through your file."

"There can't be much in it unless Cambry did a background check."

Going over to one of the chairs, she opened the folder and sat down.

After a moment he chose the chair around the corner of the table from her. "I don't understand why I'm meeting with *you.* Are you some type of patient advocate?" His gaze took in her uniform again, then returned to her face.

"No, not in the way you mean. I'm an oncology nurse and usually work with the kids. I suppose that's one of the reasons Dr. Chambers chose me to walk you through this. I can explain any aspects of the testing and the transplant, though a transplant counselor will do most of that. But I'm supposed to act as a liaison for you and Mr. Cambry—with the hospital, with the lab, with the doctors—to make sure everything gets done as quickly as possible."

"I see. Cambry told me he's a corporate attorney. I don't know that much about him except that he left the firm in Phoenix to open a branch here in Portland not so long ago. If this hospital is giving him his own personal liaison, I imagine he contributed to it already."

Leigh felt herself blushing and knew there was no reason for it. "I can't really discuss benefactors of this hospital with you."

"No, I guess you can't, not and be a good liaison."

She sensed a cynicism in Adam's attitude, and then she remembered. Actually she'd never forgotten, she'd just put it to the back of her mind. "You don't think much of hospitals and medical personnel."

Leaning back slightly, he agreed. "That's right. That hasn't changed. In fact, this is the first I've stepped into a hospital since the day Delia died."

Leigh ached for the boy who had lost his horse, his best friend in the world at age seven, as well as his sister in the same day.

"How *is* your family?" she asked gently because she felt as if she should. She'd visited the Bartlett farm a few times while she and Adam were dating. She'd seen the strain between him and Owen Bartlett, had felt the distance between him and his adoptive mother and the two sisters who had been first in their parent's hearts, especially after they'd lost Delia.

"Owen died two years ago."

"I'm terribly sorry." Then she asked a question she knew was none of her business. But she was curious about what had happened to Adam. "Had things gotten any better between you and your dad before he died?"

Silence swirled around the room until finally Adam replied, "How could they get any better, Leigh? Owen Bartlett adopted me because he wanted a boy who could do the chores and take over the farm some day. He and my mom never considered me their real son.

You know after Delia got trampled by Lancer, they blamed me for her death.''

He stopped abruptly, then continued, ''Long before Owen died, I made arrangements for someone to manage the farm for him and to do the heavy work. It gave my mom an easier life, too, and I think she appreciates that. Sharon still lives there with her, but Rena went to Australia on a trip and never came back. She's living in the Outback with a sheep rancher and Mom says she's happy.''

Leaning forward, he motioned toward his file. ''But I'm not here to talk about the past, and I'm sure you want to get on with this, too. I think Cambry said there would be special orders there for all the testing I'm to have done today.''

Politely Adam had filled her in and now he wanted to get on with the job at hand, a life-saving job. She couldn't believe she'd detoured from that. Still…seeing him again—

Mark Cambry came first.

Glancing over the information on Adam, she saw it was indeed scanty. ''Before you can get started with the testing, we have to go over the intake form. Then I'll explain what they're going to do in the lab. You'll also have a chest X-ray, and I see there's an appointment for you at three with Dr. Mason for a physical.''

Adam took his cell phone out of his inside jacket pocket. ''I didn't realize I was going to be here most of the day. Before I go to the lab, I need to make a call.''

She reached for his cell phone before he pressed

Enter. "You can't use that in here—not in the hospital."

Her hand had clasped his. His skin was warm and taut, the back of his large hand, hair roughened. Licks of fire shot up her arm as her gaze met his. She thought she saw a flicker of something old and wild there.

Pulling away from her clasp, Adam slipped the phone back into his pocket. "That's damn inconvenient."

She motioned to the phone on the credenza. "You're welcome to use that. Press eight for an outside line. If you need privacy, I can step outside."

"I don't need privacy. I'm just going to clear my schedule."

Clear his schedule of what? she wondered, then caught herself. The job of liaison wasn't to poke into Adam Bartlett's business or his life and she had to remember that.

However, during the intake session she found out exactly what Adam was doing now. She'd given him a few minutes to fill out basic information on the form. Under Occupation, he'd written—CEO of Novel Programs, Unlimited. Novel Programs, Unlimited, was a software firm that had made its mark in the United States. But whenever she saw a clip about it, the article was about product development or the latest software program. She remembered the name Dylan Montgomery being associated with it, but not Adam's name.

When she went over the information with him, she asked, "How long have you been with Novel Programs, Unlimited?"

"Did I miss filling in a blank?" he asked.

"No," she replied, not feeling as self-conscious this time. After all, she wasn't going to pretend as if she hadn't known him, hadn't dated him for three months, hadn't fallen in love and given him up for a dream that had seemed bigger and more important. "I just wondered."

After sitting there for a long moment, he laid his pen on the table. "I used that scholarship I won at the Computer Science Fair to go to Stanford. My roommate and I developed programs we felt were unique. We started our company in college and went public the summer after we graduated. The rest is history, as they say."

"Dylan Montgomery was your roommate?"

"Yes, he was. He doesn't mind posing for pictures and talking to reporters, as well as being chief financial officer."

"On the other hand, you don't like any of that," she guessed, remembering the quiet and sometimes remote teenager he'd been.

"I like publicity almost as much as I like hospitals and doctors."

"The doctor you overheard after your sister died—"

"Was an unfeeling son of a bitch. His exact words were, 'We shouldn't have wasted our time on her. I knew she was gone when they brought her in.' Even a seven-year-old could understand exactly what that meant."

"You're still bitter."

"No, Leigh. I just know where I can place my trust and where I can't. I'm only here today because there's an outside chance that I can help save Mark Cambry's life. So let's get to it, okay?''

Old hurt crept over Leigh's heart and she ached to clear the air between them. She needed to tell him why she'd broken off their relationship so long ago. She needed to try to make him understand.

Yet she couldn't do that now. It was time to give him a capsulized version of the transplant process and then escort him to the lab. She'd be checking on his progress throughout the day and maybe when he was finished…

From the file folder she took out a sheaf of papers and placed them before him. ''Let me explain what's going to happen next.''

Leigh kept the rest of their session impersonal and then she acted as the guide she was supposed to be a half hour later as they walked down the hall to the elevator.

Adam cut her a glance. ''I can find the lab on my own.''

''I have no doubt of that but this is my job for today, so let me do it.''

Silence reverberated between them as they waited for the elevator.

Finally Adam asked, ''You said you work with kids?''

''Yes, and I love it. I'm going to miss it when I leave for med school in June.''

That brought his gaze to her face. ''Where are you going?''

''Case Western in Cleveland.''

The elevator doors swished open. After they stepped

inside, silence reigned again until they walked down the first-floor hall to the laboratory door.

Leigh handed Adam three sets of papers. "Just give these to the receptionist. She'll buzz me when you're finished. Normally we hold off on the X-ray and the physical until the results come back, but Mr. Cambry is paying for all this, and if you're a match, he wants you ready to go."

"No, he won't be paying for this. *I* will."

"But my notes state—"

"I don't care what your notes state. Make sure you see to it that they're changed. My name goes to billing for these tests."

His jaw was set, his tone resolute. She could see this was important to him and something on which he wouldn't compromise. But she'd have to speak to Dr. Chambers about it and see how he wanted to handle the situation. For now she just nodded.

Adam opened the laboratory door and went inside.

Three hours later, Leigh met Adam in Dr. Mason's office after his physical had been completed. She suspected being here, letting doctors poke and prod him, had been more difficult than she could ever imagine. After they'd dated a few weeks, he'd told her how his parents had brought him to the hospital the day that Delia was rushed here in the ambulance, how he'd seen a trauma team impersonally work on Delia, how they'd attached her to tubes, put her on a ventilator. To a child, that all had to be terrifying. He'd seen all the personnel as unfeeling, mechanical, uncaring. Then when he'd heard that doctor's comments—

His face was grim now as he shrugged into his suit jacket again, then glanced at his watch.

"Still hoping to get some work in today?" she asked. She'd *hoped* they could have a cup of coffee together, and she could explain why she'd written him that note ten years ago.

"I have a conference call in fifteen minutes, but I'll be able to take it in the car."

Some of the offices led directly outside and now she walked with Adam as he opened the door and stepped into the beginning-of-March breeze. The sun was shining brightly today.

He took a deep breath, held his face up to its heat and then gave a sigh. "I don't know how you work in that place. It's so..."

"Clean?" she asked, hoping to coax a small smile from him.

Although the grim expression was gone now, he still didn't smile. "That wasn't quite the word I was searching for."

For some reason she felt she had to change his mind about this hospital and what she did. "Mark's a wonderful little boy, Adam. I cared for him during his last hospitalization. If you're a match, and if we can do the transplant, this will become a life-saving place. Can you think about that?"

At her question, she thought she saw an old tenderness come back into Adam's green eyes. She thought she felt a warmth that at one time had made her believe she belonged in a new place...made her feel as if she weren't alone.

"I *will* think about that," he said.

Then Adam Bartlett headed for the parking garage, and Leigh wondered if he'd ever give her the chance to explain why she'd left him so long ago.

Chapter Two

Adam rode Thunder at a full run in a way he'd never ridden him before. They were chasing the end of day and eluding it at the same time. As Adam leaned low, he and his horse were one. The stallion was always responsive under his hands, always tuned in to his voice.

A few years ago, when Adam had moved from a condo in the city to the ranch, the first thing he'd done was to buy Thunder—even before he'd bought furniture. Cedar Run Ranch was now his haven, and Thunder was his best friend. Part Arabian, the stallion had an intuition that told him exactly what Adam wanted…when he wanted it. Although Adam and Dylan had been friends since college, he didn't even tell

Dylan some of the worries and secrets he confided in Thunder.

Pines and cedars thickened as the brush tore and scattered under the stallion's hooves. Adam slowed him with a touch. The wind that had splashed against Adam's face became gentler, and he sat up straight on the horse's back. He was riding without a saddle, his worn jeans a thin barrier between his thighs and Thunder's sculpted muscles. He hadn't even worn a jacket, just pulled a sweatshirt over his head.

"Slower, boy," Adam suggested to the horse.

The stallion neighed in reply and Adam smiled, his first real smile since Jared Cambry had forced a meeting this morning.

After another quarter of a mile, Adam walked Thunder between moss-covered maples to the bank of a creek. Rain kept it full as it washed over rocks and rippled along the brambled bank. The sound of the water, the rustle of the leaves overhead, Thunder's black mane under Adam's hand, soothed him in a way nothing else could. Yet even that soothing couldn't make him forget Leigh Peters's big, blue eyes. Those damn big, blue eyes.

He remembered the first time they'd stopped him in his tracks. It had been the end of March, ten long years ago. He'd just been putting in time, wanting his senior year over with so he could get away from his adoptive parents' farm, go to college, make a real life. He'd walked down the high school hall, and he'd seen a girl stuffing books and a jacket into one of the senior lockers. She'd looked up when she heard his footsteps, and those eyes...

He had to admit it wasn't only her eyes. She'd had long blond hair that had fallen over her shoulders, a curvy figure that had encouraged his eighteen-year-old hormones to run wild. And she'd just looked lost.

He wasn't sure what had made him stop. He hadn't dated much. Since he was ten and built his own computer, he'd been interested in creating software programs, challenging himself with ever more difficult computer games, staying away from the crowd that went drinking every Saturday night and acted as if going steady were the be all and end all of life. He had plans to make himself into a man whom even Owen Bartlett would have to respect.

Girls had buzzed around him now and then—in the lunchroom, in the gym where he shot hoops whenever he could get a chance. Although experimenting sexually with them might have been fun, he hadn't wanted the complications or the responsibility….

Until he'd seen Leigh, and dreams and life and plans had changed. He'd walked up to her and asked her if she was new at the school. She'd seemed so grateful he'd stopped to talk to her. That's how it had begun. She'd been his first lover, his first confidante, his first hope that a bond with another person wouldn't cause pain.

But after three months of dating, she'd sent him a note. It had said she couldn't see him again and explained nothing. When he'd called her, she hadn't answered. When he'd stopped by, her mother had told him she wasn't home.

It had taken a few weeks for him to get back on track, but then he'd focused on the future again, life without Leigh, a college education that could hand him the brass ring.

Thunder neighed again and tossed his head.

"Yep, she's still beautiful," Adam acknowledged to himself and the horse.

But Leigh had obviously had a reason for walking out of his life back then, and now he didn't care what it was. He didn't care that he'd seen her again today. She was off to medical school in June, and he had Jared Cambry to deal with. All Cambry had cared about was Adam getting to the hospital for the appointed tests. They certainly hadn't had a long-lost father-and-son reunion. Cambry only cared about eight-year-old Mark.

However, Mark Cambry was Adam's half brother. Real family...blood family. Adam had been told it could be more than a week until the test results came in.

And if he was a match?

Although he despised hospitals and what they represented, he would save his brother's life.

An hour and a half later, Adam had finished his ride and groomed and fed Thunder. As he mounted the steps and crossed the porch to his log home, he thought about going back to the office to finish the work that hadn't gotten done today. He'd no sooner opened the front door, inset with a triangular beveled glass window, when his phone rang.

He crossed the wide-planked flooring, scattered with unique brightly colored wool rugs a decorator had found in a small village in Alaska. They were handwoven, and the greens, browns and blues added color to the room furnished with a supple black leather couch and armchair, as well as a sage-colored recliner. The polished pine lamps with their parchment shades, the wrought-iron tables with their glass tops blended together to make the room homey, comfortable, and tasteful. His state-of-the-art plasma-screen TV and entertainment center looked out of place in the rustic surroundings, but Adam didn't care about that.

Picking up the cordless phone beside the sofa, he answered, "Bartlett here."

"Adam, it's Leigh. Leigh Peters."

As if he didn't remember her last name.

She went on. "I managed to set up an appointment for you with the transplant counselor tomorrow."

He ran his hand through his hair. She'd mentioned she was going to do that. He just hadn't expected the appointment to be tomorrow. "That was quick."

"Would you rather I postpone the appointment for a few days? I could set it up at the end of the week instead."

Whether he was a match or not, he wanted to know more about the transplant process. He'd heard about the donor registry but had never realized what all of it meant. "What time tomorrow?"

"Marietta Watson—that's who you will be meeting with—has an opening at eleven and another at four. Which would you prefer?"

"Four would be better for me. I can go to the office early and get in a full day. I'm surprised you're still at work."

"I was waiting for Marietta to get back to me about appointment times. In the meantime, I visited with some of my patients."

She really *did* like her work. He could hear it in her voice. Suddenly he had the urge to know if she was involved with anyone, if she lived by herself or with a lover. "You don't have anyone at home waiting for you?"

There were a few beats of silence before she replied, "Yes I do—my mom. It's more economical for me to live with her while I'm saving for med school."

Relief swept through Adam, then he reminded himself he had no right to feel it. He remembered Leigh's mother, Claire. She and Leigh looked more like sisters than mother and daughter. He'd envied the close bond the two of them had shared. "I bet your mom's going to miss you when you leave."

"I'll miss her. Though, she might be glad to finally get me out of her hair."

There was affection and laughter in Leigh's voice, and Adam felt himself responding to it. He'd been Leigh's first lover, and she had been his. That was a sense of connection he couldn't deny. Yet he'd felt betrayed when she'd walked away without a word. He'd been a nobody then with nothing but hopes for a better future. Obviously she hadn't been willing to take a chance on him or else she hadn't felt the same depth of caring he had.

"Where is Marietta Watson located?" he asked, getting back to the subject at hand.

"She's on the first floor, the opposite side of the

building from Dr. Mason. I can meet you in the lobby if you'd like."

"No, that's not necessary. I'll find her. What's the suite number?"

"It's 107. If she's left for the day, I'll leave a note for her that you're coming in at four."

"Remember, Leigh, the charges for all of this go on my tab."

"I spoke with Dr. Chambers about that. He said he'd have a talk with Mr. Cambry...with your father."

It sounded ironic for Adam to hear those words. He and Cambry had parted this morning without any plans to meet again. Yet no matter what the testing revealed, Adam wanted to know more about this sister Cambry had found, too. He wanted to know more about all of it. For now, though, he'd sit tight and wait to see what happened next.

"Thanks for calling, Leigh. And thanks for setting up the appointment. Now you'd better go home and get some supper."

"Is that what you're going to do?" Her question showed obvious interest in his life and he didn't know what to make of that.

"No, I'm going to change and go back into the city. I'll pick up Chinese on the way."

"You don't live in town?"

"No. I have a ranch southwest of Portland. I needed some space around me."

"You got used to space growing up on the farm."

"I guess I did. But Cedar Run Ranch is nothing like Owen Bartlett's farm. Believe me."

"I'm glad you found a home," she said, obviously

understanding everything he'd ever felt about Owen Bartlett and his adopted family.

"You enjoy supper with your mom."

"You enjoy Chinese at your desk."

"I will. Goodbye, Leigh."

Then she said goodbye and ended the connection.

Adam switched off the phone, set it on its base, and stared at it for a long time.

Finally, shaking off the foggy fingers of time-passed, he headed for his shower, a fresh change of clothes and a night of the work that had become his life.

I'm his liaison, Leigh told herself the following afternoon as she hurried down the corridor toward Marietta Watson's office.

It was almost five o'clock and knowing from experience that the counseling sessions lasted about an hour, she'd decided to check in on Adam and see how the session had gone.

Stop kidding yourself, her subconscious whispered. *You want to see him again.*

It wasn't that she *wanted* to see him. Well, maybe she did. For reasons that had nothing to do with her being his liaison. They had unfinished business and it was time she apologized for it.

When she opened the door to Suite 107, there was no one in the small waiting room. The door was closed to Marietta's inner office, so Leigh sat down to wait. She'd no sooner picked up a year-old magazine to page through when Adam opened the door, and he and Marietta walked out. They were laughing, and Marietta—a pretty brunette a few years older than Leigh—was looking up at Adam as if she found him very attractive.

He was.

He'd always been handsome in a rugged sort of way and had never seemed to understand how that and his broad shoulders and piercing green eyes affected women. At twenty-seven, and CEO of his own company, he must have had lots of affairs. She hadn't. Life had been filled with work and study. Yet to be honest, she'd never found a man she wanted to be intimate with the way she had been with Adam.

"How did it go?" she asked, looking at Marietta's brightly colored dress, wishing she'd had a change of clothes in her locker.

After Adam gestured to Marietta, he smiled. "She's great. She could explain the theory of relativity to a first-grader and he'd understand. I now have a basic grasp of HLA typing, conditioning for the transplant recipient and an overview of the harvesting procedure."

Leigh knew they'd covered aspects other than the technical ones—what the transplant would mean to Mark, how difficult the whole ordeal would be for the boy, as well as Adam's part in it, if it came to that.

"From your questions, I knew you were processing everything I told you," Marietta concluded. "Sometimes the donors I counsel get lost in the stress and can't absorb the information I give them."

Clasping Adam's arm as if she'd known him for years, she added, "If you think of anything we didn't talk about, or if you have any other questions, feel free to call me. Now I have some paperwork to finish before I can leave.''

She raised her hand in a wave to both of them and went back inside her office and closed the door.

Adam was studying Leigh curiously as if wondering why she was there. Feeling a bit self-conscious, she explained, ''I wanted to make sure your session went smoothly.''

''So you can report to Dr. Chambers and Cambry?''

''No,'' Leigh answered patiently. ''I'm not reporting to anyone. I'm just trying to make sure everyone's needs are met.''

There was a need that suddenly flared in Adam Bartlett's eyes, and she felt heat creep into her cheeks. ''Marietta's good at her job, too. She means it when she says to call her if you have any further questions.''

''I researched bone marrow transplants on the Internet last night. That's how I was able to quickly absorb everything she said. It's certainly cut-and-dried when you get right down to it. She did explain how difficult a decision it is for parents to put their child through the ordeal. I didn't understand the implications of that before.''

Leigh nodded. ''Mr. Cambry and his wife are going through anguish that I hope I never see.''

As they both thought about that, Leigh impulsively asked, ''Would you like to come to dinner at my place?''

A few prolonged seconds passed, then Adam asked, ''Dinner's part of your job, too?''

''Dinner has nothing to do with my job. Mom's working late tonight so we can talk privately.''

He cocked his head to study her. "And what do we have to talk about?"

"I thought maybe we could...catch up. I could make pasta and a salad. I bought a loaf of Italian bread at the bakery yesterday. How about it?"

When Adam withdrew, when he decided to keep thoughts to himself, not one iota of what was going on in his head showed. That used to frustrate her, and it did now, too.

After an interminably long pause, for which she realized she was holding her breath, he finally replied. "All right. A home-cooked meal sounds good. What's your address?"

Portland General Hospital was located on the outskirts of the city. When it had been built in the 1940s, it had stood apart from the hustle and bustle. Now urban Portland had almost caught up with it. As Leigh checked her rearview mirror, she caught a glimpse of Adam's BMW as he followed her in the dusk. Her heart raced when she thought about having dinner with him. Her mind went over apologies and explanations that didn't seem to say what she wanted them to. By the time they reached the apartment complex where she and her mom lived, her palms were damp.

The apartment building, like so many of Portland's structures, was built of wood. It was small as apartment complexes went, with twelve units on three floors. There was an old Victorian house to the left of the building, a dry cleaner and bakery to the right. Checking again in the mirror to see if Adam was following her, Leigh drove around to the back where the parking lot for the apartments was located.

After Adam pulled his car in beside hers, they both got out. As they walked to the rear entrance of the building, she said, "We're on the second floor."

Adam was silent as they mounted the steps, and Leigh suddenly panicked. Maybe this wasn't such a good idea. When they arrived at the apartment door, she used her key to open it and stepped inside.

She could almost hear what Adam was thinking. The apartment wasn't any bigger than the one she and her mom had shared when she'd been in high school. It was decorated in a totally feminine way—shades of rose and yellow, flowered chintz slipcovers over an old sofa and chair, cream-and-taupe braided rugs on the painted tan floor. Prints of Monet watercolors hung on two walls in oak frames with a mirror sconce beside one of them. The television, which sat on a bookshelf, was only as large as the computer monitor that was housed with a keyboard on the hutch in the back corner of the living room.

Taking off her coat, Leigh hung it on a peg inside the front door.

After Adam shrugged out of his suit jacket, he tossed it over the armchair. Next he loosened his tie, and Leigh found it hard to swallow. He looked consummately sexy, and his green eyes followed her as she moved into the kitchen.

"You said your mom's working late tonight. Is she still a medical secretary?" he asked.

Leigh removed a spaghetti pot from a bottom cupboard. "Yes, she is. For a family practice."

Adam nodded to the computer. ''Is that yours or hers?''

''Mostly hers. I used it in nursing school. She takes in word processing and does that in her spare time.'' Her mother had worked two jobs since Leigh was twelve, saving money and adding to the medical school kitty. Leigh would never be able to repay her for all she'd done for her.

As Leigh turned on the spigot and held the pot underneath to fill it, Adam was suddenly by her side.

''I'll lift it out for you,'' he said as the pot became heavier with the water.

The kitchen area was small, the work space minuscule. Adam's arm brushed hers. She could smell his musky scent, a mixture of man and cologne...*Adam* and cologne. His body heat seemed to surround her. Or was it simply her own body temperature rising?

His sideways glance at her was meant to tell her she should let him handle the heavy pot, but she couldn't look away from him. The eye contact brought back memories of other small spaces—his old car, the janitor's closet in the school where stolen kisses had been exciting and wild.

Water poured over the side of the pot.

She licked her lips.

He seemed to lean closer.

But then he straightened, turned away and flipped off the spigot.

Leigh let go of the pot, moved toward the refrigerator, opened the door and gathered chicken breasts and vegetables. She'd sauté them, then toss them with the pasta, olive oil and garlic.

''What else can I do?'' he asked as he set the pot on the burner and turned it on, salting it.

''Do you cook?''

''Now and then. Dylan and I had a range but no oven in our apartment at college. We became adept at opening cans and mixing them. We called all the recipes Adam-and-Dylan's goulash.''

She laughed. ''Did you write any of them down?''

''Are you kidding? That was the mystery of it. We never made the same thing twice.''

''So you and Dylan are good friends?''

Adam shrugged. ''We're friends, we're partners, we know each other's likes and dislikes, what buttons not to push. But Dylan and I are very different. He likes the city and the night life and crowds and parties.''

''And you like to work after everyone else is gone and spend your spare time at your ranch.''

''You always were a quick study,'' he remarked.

She wasn't sure that was a compliment. ''I don't know about being a quick study. I've learned how to listen to the kids, or try to hear what they don't say.'' She took a sauté pan from another cupboard and set it on the stove.

When Adam unbuttoned his cuffs and rolled up his sleeves, she lost track of what she was doing. His hair roughened forearms were muscled, his gold watch masculine against his tanned wrist.

Silence pulsed awkwardly between them along with the sexual tension that had always been there.

She asked, ''So what do you have on the ranch?''

''Lots of trees,'' he responded dryly.

Smiling, she shook her head. ''Do you have animals?''

''I have a stallion named Thunder.''

Her gaze met his and she realized he'd bought a horse to make up for the one he'd lost.

''What breed?''

''Mixed. Mostly Arabian. He's a beauty, but he's spirited and restless and hard to handle sometimes, at least for anyone but me. I have a gardener who keeps the grass mowed and the weeds in check. He takes care of Thunder when I have to go out of town, but he keeps his distance from him. I suppose that's best, for his own good.''

Leigh chopped carrots on a cutting board. ''Do you go out of town often?''

''About once a month. Dylan and I take turns with that.''

She cut up onion and fennel and saw the water was almost boiling. She told herself to wait until they were both relaxed and eating to explain what had happened so many years ago, but suddenly she felt as if it were now or never.

''Adam, I've wanted to tell you—''

The lock clicked and the door to the apartment suddenly opened. Her mother came in, saying, ''I finished at work sooner than I planned. Did you see that fancy car parked in the parking lot? I can't imagine what it's doing here.''

When Claire saw Adam standing in the shadows in the corner of the kitchen, she took a step back. ''I know you, don't I? Aren't you...?''

Stepping forward, Adam stood before her mother. "Adam Bartlett. It's been a long time, Ms. Peters."

Claire's gaze took a quick appraisal of his silk tie, his quality trousers, the shirt that still had some starch. "Where did you and Leigh meet up again?" She removed her coat and hung it next to her daughter's on another peg.

Leigh noticed her mother had worn a black pantsuit today and tucked a multicolored scarf into the neck. At forty-three her blond hair had a few strands of gray but it looked like frosting. She'd had her hair permed recently, and it waved around her face attractively. She was only forty-three because she'd become a single mom at seventeen. That's why she convinced Leigh to break up with Adam. That's why she'd insisted an involvement that Leigh was too young to handle would ruin her life.

Leigh's job at the hospital required discretion. She wasn't about to tell her mother what was going on in Adam's life. Before she could respond, Adam did it for her. "I ran into Leigh at Portland General."

Claire looked at her daughter then at Adam then back at Leigh. "Well, why don't I stay out of your way. I have résumés to type up for clients. I can work on those until supper is ready."

"Mom, you don't have to make yourself scarce."

But Claire was already walking toward the computer. "I have to get the work done, honey." After she switched it on, it made a noise it had been making the past few days.

Adam went on alert immediately. "That sounds as

if your fan needs to be cleaned. Do you always keep the tower in the enclosed space?''

Clair nodded. ''Yes. Shouldn't I?''

Smiling patiently, he strode to the computer hutch and pulled out the tower from the lower cupboard. ''It needs to be cleaned, now and then, just like anything else. Do you want me to do it for you?''

''Will the machine stop running if I don't?''

''The fan keeps the unit cool so if it stops working, you're in trouble.''

''But you didn't come here for this. I don't want to impose.''

There was uncertainty on her mother's face, and Leigh knew she wondered if Adam knew what he was doing. ''Have you heard of the company Novel Programs, Unlimited, Mom?''

Clair nodded.

''Adam is the CEO.''

The expression on her mother's face was priceless, and Leigh knew Adam was enjoying her mother's astonishment.

''I won't break anything,'' he said with a grin. ''I promise.''

Chapter Three

Adam was examining research-and-development files when Dylan came into his office, coffee mug in hand. Adam knew his CFO had scheduled a meeting with distributors early this morning, and he supposed Dylan had come in to give him a report on how it had gone.

"Do you have a few minutes?" Dylan asked.

Pushing his swivel chair away from the computer, Adam faced the doorway. He couldn't concentrate on anything this morning after his dinner with Leigh and her mother last night. He might as well consult with his partner. "Sure. Everything go okay?"

"Nothing unexpected." Dylan sank into the chair across from Adam. "I tried to call you. Last night. You didn't even have your cell phone on."

"You didn't leave a message."

"No. I figured we could hash it out this morning. Were you out in the barn or something?"

Adam laughed. "If I'm not here working, then I must be in the barn?"

Dylan shrugged. "Yeah, that about sums it up. Are you telling me you weren't?"

"I wasn't."

"Did you have another meeting with your father?"

Something sharp stabbed at Adam's insides. "You mean Jared Cambry? No, I didn't have a meeting with him. I haven't heard from him. I think he only wants one thing from me, Dylan—bone marrow."

"You don't know that for sure."

"No, I don't." But from Cambry's words and actions, Adam suspected Mark was his sole concern.

"So where were you last night?" Dylan prodded. "Or are you going to be mysterious about it?"

Although Adam had told Dylan about Cambry and the testing at the hospital, he hadn't said anything about Leigh. He'd never told Dylan anything about her. "It's a long story."

"So fill me in. I've been here since 6:00 a.m. crunching numbers and I need the break."

Dylan worked as many hours as Adam did. Maybe if he told Dylan about the situation with Leigh, he could get a better perspective on it. After all, he probably wouldn't be seeing her again. What were the odds he'd be a compatible donor for Mark?

"There's a liaison at the hospital working with me and Jared Cambry to make sure the process runs smoothly. Coincidentally, I knew her in high school."

Dylan's brows rose. "Knew her?"

Adam wasn't sure exactly how much he wanted to reveal. On the other hand, Dylan had had a lot more experience with women than he had. "Yeah, knew her. We dated. I was serious, apparently she wasn't. She broke it off." His pride meant a lot to him, and that was hard to admit, but he'd always been honest with Dylan.

"Don't make me pull teeth here," Dylan pleaded with a grin. "What happened last night?" He raised his coffee mug to his lips.

"I fixed her mother's hard drive."

Dylan had been taking a sip of his coffee, and he choked.

At Dylan's expression, Adam smiled. "I had another session at the hospital and Leigh was there. Afterward she asked me to her place for dinner. She and her mom live together because she's saving money for med school. Anyway, I hadn't had a home-cooked meal in a while, so I went. Her mother came home unexpectedly and had dinner with us. The fan on her hard drive was making noise, so I cleaned it."

"That wasn't any more exciting than grooming your horse in the barn," Dylan muttered.

Adam couldn't help but laugh. "If you want exciting, you're going to have to look elsewhere."

Still, whenever he thought about Leigh, Adam *felt* excited. Whenever their arms had touched, eyes had met, the old attraction had sizzled. Claire had guided most of the conversation at dinner and he'd let her. It had been superficial, polite, entertaining. After dinner, he'd had a second cup of coffee, Leigh had walked him to the door, and that was that.

Except that *wasn't* that. He'd gotten the impression Leigh had wanted to talk to him privately, and her mother's arrival had deprived her of the chance to do that. Maybe it was for the best. Maybe the fire that licked through his blood whenever he was near her shouldn't be fueled by any more impromptu dates.

"So what did you call about last night?"

"I'm having a problem I don't quite know what to do with. It's Darlene."

Darlene was their receptionist/secretary. Adam had hired her a few months ago to replace the middle-aged woman who had been with them the past few years. Janet's husband had decided to take a job in San Diego and after a month's notice, she'd left. Darlene was quite different from Janet, in her midtwenties, a vivacious brunette who seemed to have endless energy. That's one of the reasons Adam had hired her.

"What kind of problem?"

"It's taking forever for her to do my correspondence. When I ask her if it's finished, she says she's still proofreading it. That's what spell checkers are for."

Suddenly Adam realized that Dylan might have dated a lot of women, but that didn't necessarily mean he understood them...or could read them. "Darlene likes you," he said simply.

"That's why my letters are taking forever?"

"You don't get it."

"What don't I get?"

"She tries to make them perfect. That takes a while."

Dylan still looked puzzled. ''What does she do with *your* letters?''

''She types them up and sends them out,'' Adam answered with a wry smile as he decided to enlighten his partner. ''She has a thing for you. Haven't you ever noticed how nervous she gets whenever you're around? She drops things, laughs that funny little laugh. She doesn't do that around me.''

''You *are* kidding, right?''

''No, I'm not. But it seems to me I've caught you looking in her direction more than once. Maybe it's not all one-sided.''

''I'm dating Natalie.''

''Yes, you are. Her father has a yacht. She's as beautiful as any Miss America. The difference is—I don't think she has an original thought in her head.''

''Hold back on what you think of her,'' his friend groused.

''I have been. You've been seeing her since Thanksgiving. I've been wondering why.''

Standing, Dylan set his mug on Adam's desk and went over to the window, staring at the sky. ''She likes to party, so do I.'' He turned around to face Adam. ''But she's not a sparkling conversationalist. On the other hand, I like the rush of every man looking at her when she's on my arm. She canceled our last date, though, and I haven't called her for a week. Maybe we both know our time together is over.''

When Adam's intercom buzzed, Dylan returned to staring out the window.

Adam depressed the button and asked, ''Yes, Darlene?''

"There's someone here to see you, Mr. Bartlett. A Leigh Peters. I asked if she had an appointment and she said she didn't."

Dylan was facing him now and looking at him with curiosity.

Why was Leigh here? Because last night her mother's unexpected presence had interrupted whatever conversation they might have had? Because now that he was a CEO rather than a poor kid with only a college scholarship to his name, she might be interested?

There was only one way to find out.

Speaking to his receptionist, he avoided Dylan's gaze. "I have a few minutes, Darlene. Send her back."

Expecting Dylan to leave, Adam sat back in his chair and waited, but his partner made no move to exit his office.

A few seconds later Leigh was peeking in his half-closed door. "Adam?"

The kick in his gut when he saw her made him rise to his feet. She looked too damn good. He was used to seeing her in that blue uniform, her hair tied back. Today she wore a pale green coatdress with gold buttons. The green made her eyes even bluer. Her hair, longer than shoulder length, was caught in a gold barrette over her right temple. It waved around her face looking silky and luscious, as luscious as her curves and her long graceful legs.

Stepping around his desk, Adam said easily, "Come on in, Leigh. Meet my partner, Dylan Montgomery. Dylan, Leigh Peters."

Crossing the room, Dylan extended his hand to her.

"It's nice to meet you. Adam told me you went to school together."

Her gaze shot to his as if she wondered what else he'd told Dylan. Then, with the composure she always seemed to possess, she smiled at his partner and slipped her hand from his. "It's good to meet you, Mr. Montgomery. I read the article in the financial section a few weeks ago where you were quoted quite heavily."

"For some reason I still can't understand, Adam always sends the reporters to me."

"You're much more tactful than I am," Adam explained.

"More tactful maybe, but not more knowledgeable. One of these days you're going to have to do your own PR. Speaking of PR, don't forget that cocktail party Saturday night at my condo. I mean it, Adam. You can't duck this one. I have a few guests coming who can take our fall software line into the international markets quickly."

Crossing to the door, he said, "It's nice to meet you, Miss Peters. Adam, let me know if you come up with any ideas about the problem we discussed."

When Dylan exited the office, he closed the door.

"I didn't mean to interrupt anything important," Leigh apologized. "This is my day off and if you have a few minutes, there's something I want to talk to you about."

Curious now, Adam motioned to the chair in front of his desk as he lodged a hip on the front edge. "Something about Mark Cambry?"

"Oh, no. Nothing that important. When I go to

school in June, I'll be taking the computer with me. I'd like to get Mom a new machine for her word processing, and I thought you could make the best recommendation. I don't have a lot of extra money to spend, but I want to make sure she has what she needs as well as a good word-processing program."

As Adam had indicated, Dylan was the tactful one. He himself always wanted to cut to the bottom line. "I could have given you that kind of advice over the phone."

Leigh looked down at her hands, which were folded around her purse in her lap, and then back up at him. It would have been better if he'd stayed on his side of the desk. He was too close to her here. He could smell the gardenia scent of her perfume. He remembered that was her favorite back in high school. He could also see the little trouble lines on her forehead. Worst of all, he could reach out and touch her if he wanted to.

Without any coy maneuvering, she merely said, "We didn't have a chance to talk privately last night."

"You said you wanted to catch up. We did that."

"Maybe. But we didn't clear the air, and I'd like to do that, too. I want to tell you why I wrote you that note."

"And why you wouldn't answer the phone? Why you hid in your room when I stopped by?" He told himself he just wanted to clear the air, too, not that any of it mattered now.

"You know what I came from, Adam. It had always been just me and Mom, and we never had much. Mom wanted so much more for me, and from the time that I was little, we talked about me becoming a doctor."

It was easy to recall her situation back then. ''You hadn't been able to afford med school. You couldn't get a scholarship, and loans available to you wouldn't have been enough to fund your education.''

''Right. So I was going to go to nursing school first.''

He waited.

After a small breath, she continued. ''You know how Mom watched us when we were together. She worried about me constantly when we weren't in sight. She finally admitted to me that she'd become pregnant her last year in high school and had barely been able to finish. Although she said many times that she never regretted having me, she also told me the pregnancy ruined her life. She had plans for college that never happened. Day care had always been hard to find, and the responsibility of taking care of a baby was monumental, especially since my father left town. He was the same age she was and not ready for the burden of a baby.''

Leigh seemed to hesitate, as if she was choosing her words carefully. ''Mom saw the two of us together, the way we looked at each other, the way we held hands, and she didn't want what happened to her to happen to me. She wanted me to have all the schooling I needed to get without any encumbrances. She especially wanted me to live my dreams because she'd had to give up hers. Mom has always done so much for me, working two jobs for as long as I can remember. When she advised me to stop seeing you, it seemed the best thing to do.''

While Adam studied her, she didn't look away or

duck her head, and he respected that. ''Why didn't you tell me all this then? Why the note?''

''I knew if I saw you again, I wouldn't be able to break it off. We were young, Adam, so young. Mom kept pointing that out. You had won first prize in that computer science fair and gotten a scholarship and Mom was worried about *you,* too. She didn't want me to hold you back, either.''

Nothing would have held him back. He would have liked to have taken Leigh along with him, but she'd had other plans, other dreams and maybe now, seeing the success he had made of his life, she regretted that.

His intercom beeped again, and he realized he hadn't told Darlene to hold his calls. When he pressed the button on the intercom, she said, ''Jared Cambry on line two.''

This was shaping up to be some morning.

Leigh started to get up from her chair as if to leave to give him privacy, but Adam shook his head, indicating that he wanted her to stay as he took the call. ''Mr. Cambry, has something happened with Mark?''

''No, nothing's happened with Mark. And it's Jared, Adam.''

First names was progress, Adam supposed. ''All right...Jared. If you're calling to see if the testing is completed, it is.''

''I knew it was. Leigh Peters called me.''

''I see.''

''I wanted to thank you for going through with it.''

''No thanks are necessary,'' Adam said in a low voice. He might not be a match.

After a moment of silence, Jared explained, ''Mark asked me to call you. He'd like to meet you.''

''We might not match,'' Adam said aloud now.

''He knows that. We've discussed as much as we can with him every step of the way. He's having one of his better days today, and you were on his mind this morning.''

''You want me to meet him today?''

''I know this is another imposition, but these days we try to give Mark whatever he asks for...whatever we can. Would it be possible for you to clear your schedule this morning?''

Glancing down at the printout Darlene had laid on his desk earlier, he saw there wasn't anything listed that couldn't be postponed. She could juggle his appointments and he could take care of the rest later today.

''Give me your address,'' Adam decided. He wasn't surprised when the location of Cambry's home was in a section of town where the elite lived. ''I'll be there in half an hour.''

When he settled the handset on the console once more, he turned to Leigh. ''Mark wants to meet me. I'm going to go over there now.''

''You'll like Mark. He's mature beyond his years. Mr. and Mrs. Cambry are very open with him about everything. I wonder how he's doing with all this waiting.''

''You mean physically?''

''Yes.'' Her blue eyes were worried and concerned. ''If you want to keep this private, I'll understand. But

I could come along with you to assess his condition, to look at how he's doing as a medical professional.''

''Would this be part of your job as liaison?'' He didn't know Leigh anymore and he wasn't sure of her motives.

''That's part of it, but there's more. I'd like to put our past behind us. I thought maybe we could be friends.''

As Adam turned over her words in his mind, he couldn't help but be wary. All the relationships in his past had not led him to trust easily. On the other hand, maybe he was looking at this too deeply. Leigh's expertise would be valuable when he visited Mark, and having her along might ease the awkwardness between him and the Cambrys. He had no idea what to expect when he walked in the door.

''If you have the time, I'd appreciate your coming along. Give me a few minutes to speak to Dylan and my secretary, then we can go.''

The drive to the Cambrys was quiet for the most part, and Adam was absolutely aware of Leigh sitting straight in the leather seat, not very far from him. He wondered what she was thinking about all this, whether she was sorry she was caught in the middle of it, or if she saw it simply as an opportunity to stretch her job a little.

She's going to be a doctor, a smart voice inside of his head told him again, as if to stop him from wondering anything about her. Hating that subconscious voice, he thought about Mark instead. Before he and Leigh had left Novel Programs, Unlimited, he'd snatched up one of his cutting-edge laptop computers that only weighed two pounds and a handful of sample disks, stashing all of it into a carrying case. He didn't know if Mark would enjoy the computer games or not, but trapped in bed he might appreciate something to do, not only now but later if he had to go to the hospital again.

Adam didn't want to think about what it would mean if he wasn't a match.

The area of Portland in which Jared Cambry lived was on the way to Adam's ranch. However, when Adam veered off the main road, he took a series of turns that led him past huge estates where chauffeurs, maids, butlers and gardeners were commonplace.

The Cambrys' driveway was a long curved one, lined with pines that added to the sense of privacy. Their house was exceedingly large, Tudor with its wood beams and stucco. It was a traditional house and Adam wondered if Jared Cambry had turned into a traditional man. Maybe Adam would find out something about him today in his own environment.

Adam automatically went around to Leigh's side of the car and helped her out. Her hand felt small, delicate and warm in his. She was wearing an off-white wool coat over her dress and was every inch a lady…always had been. The sun was shining again today though rain was predicted for the rest of the week. Rain in Portland in March was a given. Thoughts of rain got lost as he watched yellow sunbeams play in Leigh's blond hair, making it glisten. He felt himself responding to the feel of her skin under his, the scent of her perfume brought to him on the breeze, the concern in her large blue eyes.

"Are you ready for this?" she asked gently.

"As ready as I'm going to be."

Releasing her hand, he opened the door to the back and pulled out the computer case.

Adam walked the curving path to the door beside Leigh, taking in the huge casement windows, the gables, the pristine outward appearance of everything. At the double-wide, heavy wood doors, he rang the bell.

A few moments later, Jared Cambry was at the door inviting them into the large foyer. A pretty, dark-haired woman, petite and slender, with chin-length wavy hair, came to greet them, too.

Jared dropped his arm around her shoulders. "Leigh, you've met my wife Danielle. Adam, this is my wife."

As Danielle moved closer, Adam could see the circles under her eyes, the paleness of her skin, the worry lines creasing her forehead. He imagined she'd had many sleepless nights and long days of turmoil.

Still, she touched Leigh's arm briefly, and when he extended his hand to her, she put hers in his. "I'm so glad to meet you, Adam. We can't thank you enough." Her voice caught.

Adam had known this meeting would be difficult, but he'd expected awkwardness to come from different reasons than emotion. He didn't want their thanks. He hadn't done anything.

Taking a step back, he lifted the computer. "I brought Mark something. Even if he already has a computer, this one will be chock-full of games and an e-mail program.''

''He has a PlayStation,'' Jared said. ''We haven't gotten him a computer yet, though there's a hookup for one in his room. I have one in my home office, and he can link into my Internet service. He'll probably love it. He's spending most of his days in bed.''

Jared's arm was still around his wife, and Adam could tell they were holding on to each other for support.

''Would you like to see him now?'' Danielle asked. ''He was watching TV when I went up a little bit ago. I'll make some coffee. Leigh, would you like to join me in the kitchen?''

He understood Danielle's intent at the invitation. As Adam followed Jared up the stairs, he was suddenly grateful a crowd wouldn't be around when he met Mark.

The oak steps were plushly carpeted down the middle. The house was tastefully decorated in taupes and mauves with a touch of green here and there. Jared took him to the second door on the right in the upstairs hall.

When he opened it, Adam assessed the room in a second—several posters of Harry Potter, a red-white-and-blue spread with baseballs and bats andcatchers' mitts, a television set on the dresser facing the bed. There were bookshelves not only lined with books, but with replicas of dinosaurs in porcelain, resin and plush. It was definitely a boy's room, and when Adam's gaze met Mark's in the double bed, his heart tripped, and he understood they were connected in a very big way by blood—their father's blood.

Mark was pale, so very pale. His dark-brown hair was straight and spiky, his green eyes the same color as his father's. What stunned Adam most was that Mark looked like he had when he was a boy. If someone had put their eight-year-old pictures together, Adam didn't know if a stranger could tell them apart.

Royal-blue sheets were folded at Mark's waist and he was propped up on three pillows. In spite of that, he sat up straight, glanced at his father and back at Adam. ''You're my brother?''

Adam moved into the room and sat on the corner of the bed so that he and Mark were almost at eye level. ''It seems like that may be the case. We'll know for certain after the bloodwork results are in.''

Mark was studying Adam's face. ''You're my brother. I can tell. You look like me.''

Adam laughed. ''Yep, I've got to admit, there is a resemblance. You have another older brother, don't you?''

''Yeah, but Chad looks like Mom. So does Shawna. I'm the only one who looks like Dad.''

As if the talking had tired him, Mark leaned back against the pillows.

Realizing Jared had left him alone with the boy, Adam set the computer on the bed and unzipped the case. ''I brought you something. The battery will stay charged up to ten hours and you can use this while you're in bed. From the looks of it,'' he pointed to the Harry Potter posters and the dinosaurs, ''you'll like this new game we've developed. Dino-land.''

"I can use it in bed? That's great. I get tired really fast now if I sit at my desk to draw."

Adam glanced at the corner desk and the colored pens and pencils scattered there. "So drawing's a hobby of yours?"

The boy nodded.

"I'm sure I can dig up a program to use on the computer for drawing. It'll be different than doing it by hand."

"That's okay. Anything's good to make the time pass faster. I hate being stuck up here. I hate not going to school. I hate being different from everybody else."

At that moment Adam was sure Leigh could handle this conversation much better than he could. "Do you talk about any of that with your parents?"

Mark shook his head vigorously. "No, they're so worried most of the time. Mom cries…so does Shawna. Chad and Dad just get this look on their faces. After Lissa wasn't a match, Mom's eyes were red for days until the P.I. found you. Did that lady at the hospital talk to you about the transplant?"

"You mean Marietta?"

"Yeah, she's the one. She's cool. She tried to make it sound not too scary. Did she do that for you, too?"

With a smile, Adam nodded. He knew if they went through with the transplant, this was going to be a whole lot harder for Mark than it was for him, that conditioning would involve chemo until all the abnormal bone marrow cells were destroyed. Mark would have to be in isolation before and after, and that was going to be hard on him. Yet Adam could sense this boy had spirit and that would get him through, along with the love of his family.

"How would you like it if I loaded some of these games onto the computer and you can try them out? We can make sure they work before I leave."

"I'd like that."

While Adam worked on the programs, he and Mark talked. Mark asked him where he grew up, and Adam told him about the farm, but not about his family life there.

"I've always wanted a horse," Mark confided.

"I have a horse. His name's Thunder and he's hard to handle, but he's just right for me. I've been thinking about getting a couple more. My partner says he'd come riding if I found a horse that wouldn't run away with him."

Mark laughed, and Adam felt satisfied that he could *make* him laugh. This little boy needed all the smiles and happy thoughts he could get.

"If you get more horses, can I come ride after this is all over?"

All over. *If* he was a match. They wouldn't know if the transplant was successful for two to four weeks. After that, it could be six months to a year for real recuperation. Looking into his half brother's eyes, Adam felt the hope there. Mark had to believe this would be all over and that he would be well again.

"You can come out to the ranch as soon as you're up to it. But in the meantime, when I do buy more horses, I'll take photos and scan them into the computer. I'll be able to e-mail them to you."

"Way cool!"

Adam loaded another disk.

"If you can e-mail me photos, does that mean you can just e-mail me, too?"

"If you'd like me to."

"Especially when I go back into the hospital, it would be nice. Family's great, but they just don't get Harry. And they can't tell a tyrannosaurus from a brontosaurus."

"And you think I can?"

"Can't you?" Mark challenged.

Dinosaurs had fascinated Adam when he was a kid, too. He'd haunted the school library for information and pictures about them. And as far as Harry Potter went, he had to be up-to-date on all the latest kids gimmicks and games and interests in order to create new software for them.

"I think you're older than eight," Adam decided with a chuckle.

Mark shrugged. "Mom says I'm an old soul, whatever that means."

"It means you're grown-up past your years."

"Were you grown-up past your years?"

Adam felt as if he'd always been an adult. "I guess I was."

Although he had been leaning against the pillows, now Mark sat up again. "Adam?" he asked, in a voice that urged Adam's gaze to meet his.

"What, Mark?"

"I think you're going to be a match."

Chapter Four

A short time later, when Leigh joined Adam in Mark's room, he was grateful. There were too many feelings ricocheting inside, and he needed time to sort them out. Mark was a terrific kid, and when Adam thought about the odds of them actually being a match…

As Adam loaded the last program into the computer, he could tell Leigh wasn't just talking to Mark, she was observing him and assessing him—a touch of her hand on the eight-year-old's skin, a closer look into his eyes, a few questions about how tired he was and if he'd slept last night.

Finally Adam stood and set the computer on the desk. After he plugged into the phone jack, he turned to Mark. "All set. This has an extra-long cord so it'll reach to the bed if you want to do e-mail there or surf the Net.''

''Thank you, Adam,'' Mark replied solemnly.

Adam couldn't help going to the boy then. ''I have more computers lying around the office than I know what to do with. You'll put this one to good use. But for now, I think you'd better rest.''

Leigh stood and smiled at Mark. ''That's a very good idea.''

''When will I see you again?'' Mark asked Adam.

The question tugged at Adam and he realized he truly did have a brother now. ''I'll e-mail you tonight to make sure everything's working, and I'll stop by in a couple of days.''

''Do you play chess?'' Mark asked him.

''I used to. I'm probably rusty now.''

''Dad's been teaching me. Maybe we could do that.''

''Maybe we can. Now remember you're test driving some of those programs for me. You remember what you like most about them and what you like least.''

Leaning over, Adam ruffled Mark's hair. ''I'll see you soon.'' Then he left the room.

After Leigh said her goodbyes, she caught up to him on the stairs.

''How did it go?'' she asked as he let her descend the steps in front of him.

''In some ways I see myself in him when I was a kid.''

She glanced over her shoulder at him. ''Did you connect?''

''Yes, I guess you could say we did. I've never been

around kids much, but we didn't have any trouble talking.”

As they arrived at the bottom of the stairs, Jared came to meet them. “Did he take to the computer?”

Standing there, Adam looked for himself in Jared. He found resemblance but decided it might be wishful thinking. “He seemed to. I think he likes the idea of e-mailing.”

“I let him e-mail his grandparents on my computer sometimes.”

An uncomfortable silence fell over the foyer, and Jared motioned toward the dining room and kitchen beyond. “Danielle made coffee and has some pastries. Come on.”

Adam couldn't seem to find anything to say to Jared as they made their way to the kitchen. He didn't feel like the man's son. He certainly didn't feel comfortable in his house.

Jumping in to fill the breach, Leigh spoke to Danielle as soon as she saw her in the kitchen. She was standing at an island arranging pastries on a dish. Maple cupboards were polished to a high sheen, and the ceramic tile floor and counter surfaces were immaculately clean. “Your house is beautiful. There are so many lovely touches. I especially like that sculpture of the mother and children on the buffet in the dining room.”

“That's my favorite piece, too. Jared bought it for me when I had Mark.” She took a deep breath and cleared her throat. “How do you think he's doing, Leigh? He has a doctor's appointment tomorrow but I worry every minute.”

"I know you do. I think he's doing as well as can be expected. The doctor can tell you more. How's his appetite?"

"Almost nonexistent. The housekeeper's been making him homemade puddings, fruit smoothies, doctoring up the protein drinks, anything to tempt him. Sometimes it works, but sometimes it doesn't." She looked at Adam. "Waiting to hear if you're a match or not is so incredibly difficult."

"I can only imagine."

After they were all seated at the table, Jared sipped at his black coffee then set down the mug. "Lissa will be returning from her honeymoon soon."

"You said the family who adopted her had a vineyard. Does she work there?"

"Yes, that's how she met her husband. They brought Sullivan in as a consultant to help get the vineyard in the black again."

"Do you have a number where I can reach her when she returns?"

Jared took out his wallet and slipped out a card. "This is her cell phone number. I have it on my Rolodex and on the computer, too, so I don't need this." He slid the card across the table to Adam, and Adam picked it up.

Danielle, who had been busying herself getting more coffee, making sure she had enough pastries, came around the table and put her hand on Adam's shoulder. "Lissa is a wonderful young woman. She wanted to find you as much as Jared, not only for Mark but because you're her brother."

After a few moments as Adam savored the idea of

a blood sister—a twin—Danielle moved to sit beside her husband. Glancing at him, she addressed Adam again. ''Feel free to stop by whenever you'd like. I'm sure Shawna and Chad would like to meet you, too.''

''Do they spend much time with Mark?'' He wondered if this family really cared about each other, or if everyone went their separate ways.

''Shawna and Chad both have cut back on their extracurricular activities. They take turns sitting with Mark. We're trying to keep their lives as normal as possible, but that's hard. Shawna turns sixteen in a week and a half. That's important to us, and I don't want her to feel as if we've forgotten about her in our concern for Mark.''

It was difficult for Adam to read Jared but he had no doubt that Danielle was a loving, caring mother. Even though the Cambrys were wealthy, it seemed Danielle was a hands-on parent.

Suddenly there was a buzz on the intercom. Pushing her chair back, Danielle went to it quickly. ''Yes, honey.''

''Can you bring me a glass of juice with ice in it?''

''Sure can. I'll be right up.'' Already taking a glass from the cupboard, she offered, ''I'm going to take Mark a snack, too, and see if he'll eat. Can I get either of you anything else?''

With a shake of his head, Adam pushed himself up from the table. ''No, we'd better be going.'' His gaze caught Jared's. ''Thanks for inviting me over to meet Mark.''

Jared rose to his feet. After goodbyes to Danielle,

Leigh slipped on her coat and they all walked to the door.

Jared opened it. He said to Leigh, "If you see Christopher, thank him for all his help in this. I know we'll get results from the tests quicker because he's pushing."

Moments later Jared closed the door.

Adam was silent as he strode to the car. Leigh had always had this quiet way about her that made it easy to be with her. He was grateful for that now, grateful she wasn't trying to engage him in conversation. She wasn't asking questions he didn't have answers to.

Once they were buckled in, he started the engine and turned in the circular driveway, heading away from the house.

Leigh shifted toward him. "If you're a match, will you go through with the extraction of bone marrow?"

"Of course I will. How could I not?"

"Some people would think of themselves first, the discomfort, the whole situation they'd rather get away from rather than be part of. Especially in your case, with what happened to your sister—"

"Somehow I have to erase those memories of what happened with Delia. I was a kid then. Maybe I took it all in differently from how I would have as an adult. But I'll tell you one thing. The doctors at Portland General had better be kind to Mark. They'd better not treat him like a number, because I'll be there to make sure they don't."

As they came to a T in the road, he suddenly felt the urge to be at his ranch and to show it to Leigh. "How would you like to see my place? I think I need to breathe in hay and pine before I go back to work today.'' He glanced at her. ''Unless you have plans for the rest of the day.''

''No plans. I have to run some errands this afternoon, but I'll have plenty of time for that.''

In the close quarters of the car, Adam keenly recognized his attraction to Leigh, the sexual tension that always simmered between them. He wasn't sure why he wanted to show her the ranch, but he just did.

As Adam drove southwest of the city, Leigh knew she was making a mistake. Going along with him to see Mark had been a mistake. She was as drawn to Adam Bartlett now as she had been at seventeen. He'd obviously matured. He was more broad-shouldered now, his face more angular, his hair a shade darker. There was a confident air about him now, too, that hadn't been there as a teenager. His business was a roaring success. Of course he was confident! He'd never talked about his feelings easily, but now he was definitely more guarded. Was it just around her, or was it with everyone?

She didn't have the right to ask or to meddle. After all, she wasn't going to get involved. She was involved professionally but wouldn't be involved personally.

So why was she going to his ranch with him?

Because she was curious.

It wasn't long until they'd turned off the main road onto the secondary roads. She and Adam had veered onto a lane that was much different from the winding, pristine one at Jared's house. This one wasn't bordered by trees but rather was open to the ranch's scenery with white fencing, two red barns—one larger than the other—and meadows. There were clusters of trees, mostly alders and maples, with groves of firs here and there. When they came upon the house, a shiny blue pickup truck was parked in the driveway. As Adam pulled up beside it, Leigh saw that his log home fit in with the rest of the landscape perfectly down to the split-rail fence along the walk to the front door. The house was rustically charming.

"How long have you lived here?" she asked.

"Three years this summer. After living on the farm, I thought I'd never want to see one again. But after college, Dylan and I moved into a condo in the city. I felt like I was living in a hermetically sealed bubble. I could see the sky but couldn't touch it. I could see the grass and trees below but not smell them."

"And you can touch the sky out here?" she asked with a smile.

"I guess I'm able to touch the sky when I feel free. When I can look up into the blue and the wind's on my face and there aren't any walls around me," he said, looking uncomfortable. "I've never explained it quite like that before."

"I know what you mean about walls. I love what I do, especially taking care of children. Yet sometimes I work a double shift and can't wait to get outside."

"There's a gloom about hospitals," Adam muttered as he walked up onto the porch.

"We're trying to change that at Portland General," Leigh assured him. "It has to do with the colors on the walls, decorations, less-clinical uniforms. Especially for the kids."

"That might help some." But Adam sounded doubtful as he opened his front door.

When Leigh entered Adam's house, she saw there was certainly no gloom there. The skylight in the dining room added to the daylight already pouring through the windows. Warm wood tones were everywhere, from the rustic walls and beams, to the floor and entertainment center. Colorful rugs brightened the atmosphere even further. She could see Adam's sneakers peeking out from behind the hassock and an empty soda can sitting on the side table. Last night's paper was strewn on one end of the sofa as if he'd looked at it quickly.

"This is beautiful, Adam. You must enjoy spending time here."

"It seems as if I'm always running in and out. I have a state-of-the-art kitchen I hardly ever use."

Turning to her right, she glimpsed pine cupboards, gleaming off-white counters, stainless steel appliances. Had *women* ever cooked in this kitchen? Certainly more than a few had spent the night. She suddenly wanted to know about that...wanted to know about him. But she didn't have any right to ask about other women.

"Do you want to take a walk?" he asked looking down at her black flats.

"Yes. These shoes are comfortable."

"I'll keep you out of the mud," he said with a smile and a twinkle in his eyes.

That twinkle had been absent since their first meeting on Monday. Now her heart raced faster when she saw it again.

Adam's arm brushed hers as they walked across the paved lane to one of the corrals. Suddenly, though, they were confronted with a stream of water three feet wide that flowed at least a quarter of a mile down the lane.

"We could walk around it." Adam's smile was roguish and his eyes were devilish as he added, "Or..." Picking Leigh up into his arms, he easily took a long step over the water.

"What are you doing?" Leigh gasped as she held on.

"Getting you to the other side quicker. It's pretty muddy where the water's running. I thought we'd try to save those shoes."

With her arms around Adam's neck, she breathed in the remembered male scent. Now expensive cologne mingled with it but he was the same. His beard line was starting to show and she remembered how, by the end of the school day, he'd always had a shadow. It had been sexy then and was still sexy now. His arms were strong as he seemed to hold her without any trouble at all, as if she didn't weigh 110 pounds, as if carrying her was the most natural thing in the world.

However, he only took a few steps with her, then set her down. She looked up at him and turned away, facing the corral, unable to tell what was in his eyes or on his face. Her heart was still beating so fast from the effect of him holding her so close that she could hardly catch her breath. He didn't seem likewise affected.

"This is Thunder's corral."

A beautiful black horse, at least seventeen hands high, ran with his tail flying as he caught sight of Adam. He made a circle around the corral and then another, coming to a standstill under a maple. Then he pawed one hoof onto the ground and came running to meet his master.

Adam laughed. ''It's never simple with you, is it?''

Slipping a roll of hard candy from his pocket, Adam peeled one off, and held it out in his hand to the horse. Thunder lapped it up and tossed his head, then came a little closer.

''Can I pet him?'' Leigh asked.

Adam seemed to think about that. Then he nodded. ''Slowly, very slowly, let him smell your hand. If he backs away, then we'll forget it. He definitely likes some folks better than others, and no one ever goes into the corral with him except me.''

''Is he dangerous?''

''No, not when handled correctly. But he's a stallion and he's young and he's spirited. That could lead to trouble even with someone he knows.''

Slowly Leigh held her hand out to Thunder. He didn't back away, just eyed it, and then her. ''Hold still,'' Adam murmured, his voice soft and gentle as it gave her a chill up her spine—an excited little chill.

The horse's breath blew warm on her hand and then he snuffled her fingers. When he rubbed the side of his muzzle against her palm, Adam murmured, ''Just stroke his neck.''

Thunder stood perfectly still as her fingers rippled through his coat. Then he backed up and took off at a run again.

With a chuckle, Adam acknowledged, ''He likes you. That's his way of showing off for you.''

They watched the horse as he streaked across the corral catty-corner.

''How often do you ride him?''

''On weekends for sure. With days growing longer, I'll get more riding time in during the week, too. I'd like to get a couple more horses.''

As she glanced around, she saw space wasn't a problem. Yet with Adam's schedule... ''Do you have time for that? I mean, they take a lot of care, don't they?''

''I'd make the time.''

Suddenly Adam turned and leaned against the fence. Studying her, he asked, ''What do you do in your time off, except for running errands?''

His smile had always made her tummy somersault, and now was no exception. ''You have to promise not to laugh if I tell you.''

''I won't laugh,'' he assured her.

''I go ice skating over at the mall. I've loved it ever since I was a kid. After we moved here from the Midwest, it was probably what I missed most—the frozen lakes. In another life, I might have been a figure skater,'' she teased.

In another life...if she hadn't ended their relationship...if she hadn't wanted to be a doctor...

She was looking up at him now, not at the scenery, not at the magnificent forest, not at the mountains in the distance, not at the blue sky. Adam's eyes had always told her that there were depths to him that nobody knew, and she'd always wanted to explore those depths. The times they'd made love were filled with some adolescent awkwardness. But more than that, she remembered the passion in Adam, the way he'd always tried to satisfy her first. They'd even read a book together about it—

"Leigh," he said hoarsely, and she knew he was remembering, too.

His hand slid under her hair as he nudged her closer. The scent of grass and pine and early spring hovered all around her. Her eyelids fluttered closed as his mouth came down on hers.

There was no coaxing gentleness in the kiss, no get-to-know-you-again slowness, no hesitation to make sure she wanted it, too. There was a surety in Adam now, a command that had never been there before. The kiss was a challenge, too, daring her to taste desire with him again.

She'd forgotten all about the taste of desire and how intoxicating it could be. Kisses came and went, but with Adam…

Adam's kiss had always been like a shimmering rainbow filled with so many colors it dazzled her until she got lost in its brilliance. He didn't just kiss her. His tongue slipped into her mouth and he explored her. He savored her. He remembered her. Although she felt terrifically off balance, although her feet didn't really seem to be touching the earth, although the world as she knew it faded away, she was all too aware of everything about Adam. His muscles tensed as they kissed, his body becoming even harder. The taut strength in his arms was evident in the rest of his body as he brought her closer into him, as she felt his thigh muscles against her skirt, as her breasts pushed against his chest. As he grew harder, she felt herself growing softer, molding into him, molding to him.

When the wind picked up and blew through her hair, her arms went around Adam's neck to hold on, to keep her from floating away.

Then abruptly his hands were on her arms, and he was backing away, breaking the kiss, ending it.

When she gazed up at him, she expected to see passion in his eyes, tenderness, something she'd recognize. But she saw nothing. They weren't mirrors to the soul, but simply shuttered windows that didn't reveal anything inside the man.

He didn't appear to be the least bit affected by what had happened when he said, "For old-time's sake."

She wanted to hear some humor in his voice and warmth, something. But it was unemotional, factual, unfeeling even. She felt like a fool.

"Why did you do that, Adam?"

"To see if my memories were true or figments of my imagination."

"It was an experiment?" she asked, angry now and not sure why.

"You could say that. Admit it, Leigh, you were as curious as I was. Otherwise you would have backed away."

He'd hit *that* nail on the head. How could she be angry at him for acting on what she'd been thinking? Still she wasn't angry about him kissing her. She was annoyed that he hadn't felt anything when he had.

Trying to prove to herself otherwise, trying to prove

that his world had shaken a little, too, she asked, "So was your curiosity satisfied?"

"It was."

And that seemed to be all he was going to say on the subject. She wasn't going to poke and prod at him to see if he'd felt sparks and fire, too. "Well, I'm glad. Kissing for experimentation sake will definitely further the study of man-woman relationships." She was babbling and she knew it but she didn't care. Adam's kiss had rattled her much more than she wanted to admit.

Adam glanced at his watch. "We'd better be getting back."

She'd already told him she didn't have that much to do today so it wasn't *her* schedule he was worried about. After all, he was an important CEO. He had responsibilities, duties and a schedule to keep.

Turning away from the corral, she started across the lane and was met by the wide band of water. She was feeling disgruntled, flustered, embarrassed by giving in to an impulse that meant nothing to him. She wasn't about to have him watch her walk the whole way around the water. She also wasn't going to let him carry her across it again. No way, no how. There was only one course to take.

As she slipped off her shoes, she found a spot where she could see the mud halfway across the water. Shoes in hand, she took a leap on to the mound and felt her feet squish down into the brown ooze. Not giving a hoot about that at this point, she jumped clear of the water onto the lane, hurried to the grass and wiped her feet off in it. Taking a tissue from her pocket, she finished wiping her feet the best she could and slipped them back into the shoes, pretending there weren't splashes of mud on her nylon hose.

Adam had leaped over the stream of water effortlessly and was now watching her. She didn't look at him as she balled the tissue, stuffed it into her pocket and then took off toward his car.

With a few long strides he caught up to her and clasped her arm. "Leigh?"

Stopping, she looked up at him. She couldn't quite tell if he was suppressing a smile around the corners of his mouth. The mouth that had taken her back…taken her forward…

"On Saturday night Dylan is giving a cocktail party, and he insists I bring a date. How would you like to go along?"

She should say no. He was making it clear that this was a business event and he needed someone along because that was the proper thing to do.

But maybe he *had* felt something when he'd kissed her. Maybe…

"I might stop in to see Mark again, too, and it would give us a chance to discuss his condition."

So much for maybes. Dr. Chambers had given her the order to be available to Adam as well as Jared and his family. She'd forget about the kiss and go for the experience of the party. She'd also be doing her job as liaison. It had been a long time since she'd gotten all dressed up. In fact, she suspected she'd never been to a party quite like the one Dylan Montgomery would throw.

"A cocktail party sounds like fun. What time should I be ready?"

Chapter Five

On Saturday when Adam visited Mark, the little boy seemed weaker and paler to him. Because of that, Adam kept his visit short. The eight-year-old was almost asleep when he left.

Adam had just closed Mark's bedroom door when a teenager came running up the steps. She had dark-brown, perfectly straight hair that went to her shoulders, and bangs that fell nearly to her eyes.

Spotting him, she came up short, then mounted the last three steps more sedately.

"You must be Adam," she guessed with a quick smile, reminiscent of Danielle's.

"Yes, I am. You must be Shawna." Adam extended his hand, and she shook it without hesitation as if she was used to meeting adults every day of the week. She was wearing jeans that had their share of holes for effect and a lime-green T-shirt under a crocheted sweater.

With a glance at Mark's door, she asked, "How is he today? I left early this morning before he was up. Mom was out back talking to a neighbor when I came in."

When Adam had arrived earlier, Danielle had told him Jared was at work today. He tried to bring his work home, but some things he just couldn't.

"Mark tired quickly," Adam said honestly.

Shawna sighed and her eyes became moist. "Some days are like that—more and more days. I wish there was something *I* could do for him. I wish I had been a match."

When he'd met with the counselor, Marietta Watson had told him she'd had a few sessions with Shawna and Chad as well as their parents. The situation was difficult for siblings, too. "For some reason you weren't. But you can hope with me that I am."

"Hope with you." Closing her eyes for a moment, Shawna leaned against the banister. "That's kind of nice. Mom goes to church a lot more now to pray, but I can't see that going and saying a bunch of prayers will help anything. I know how to hope, though."

"Then, in your way, you're praying." Not that Adam was an expert at it. He hadn't prayed in years. But the situation with Mark had made him look outward to something much larger than himself.

Shawna didn't seem in a hurry to go into Mark's room or to end their conversation, and Adam wondered if she needed somebody besides Marietta to talk to about all this, too. ''I hear you're going to be sixteen soon.''

She gave a little half shrug. ''Yeah. Mom and Dad are having a party for me and everything. But it doesn't seem right somehow…with Mark sick.''

''Turning sixteen is something to celebrate. I'm sure your parents are proud of you, and they want to show you that.''

''Maybe. Later today after Dad gets home, Mom wants to go shopping with me for an outfit. She hardly ever leaves Mark now, and I don't know if I want her to go. If something happened—''

''That's why man made cell phones,'' Adam said with a smile. ''I'm sure your mom has one.''

Shawna smiled back. ''Yeah, she does. I told her I wanted one for my birthday. I told her I'd be responsible with it. Then I could call in and check how things are going.''

Simply in the short while he'd talked to Shawna, Adam had no doubt she *would* be responsible with it. ''Mark said you'd been helping him get my e-mails.''

''I hope you don't mind that I read them.'' Her face flushed slightly. ''But if he's really tired, I download them, then read them to him.''

''I don't mind. Do you type in his messages to me?''

She nodded. ''He does it himself during the day, or I guess he gets Mom to help. I hope he's not e-mailing you too much. We don't want him to bother you.''

At work Adam checked his e-mail often, and if he had a message from Mark, he responded immediately.

They'd gone back and forth three or four times a day since he'd given him the computer.

"He's not bothering me. He can e-mail as often as he likes."

Shawna's gaze passed over Adam's rugby shirt, his jeans, his athletic shoes. "*We're* related, too," she said as if just realizing it.

"Yes, we are. I'm your half brother."

"That sounds silly—half brother, Lissa's half sister. It seems to me you either are or you aren't."

Adam couldn't help but smile at that.

When she saw it, she added, "Well, it's true. When Dad first told us about all this, I was real…real disappointed in him. If I ever dated a boy who got me pregnant and then took off, Dad would want to kill him."

Adam supposed that was probably true.

"Aren't you mad at him?" she prodded.

Maybe he *was* downright, bottom-out angry at Jared. "I haven't had very long to sort it out. Think about how you felt the day your dad told you the whole story."

"Yeah, that was confusing. I could see Mom was upset about all of it but trying not to be. In another way…we were all glad about it because there was more hope for Mark. Do you know what I mean?"

"I know *exactly* what you mean. Probably the reason I haven't sorted it out yet is because I'm thinking about Mark and not much else."

"The waiting is so hard." Shawna looked down at her hand as she rubbed it along the banister.

"I know it is."

Then she looked up, her face suddenly brighter. "I'm going to hope along with you. I'm going to tell Mom and Dad that's what we all should do." She looked at Mark's door again. "Well, I'd better go. I can sit with him even if he's sleeping."

Halfway to Mark's bedroom, she stopped and turned. "Can you come to my birthday party?"

"Are you sure it isn't just for—"

"Family?" she finished with a smile. "You *are* family. It's next Saturday at seven. Will you come?"

It seemed to mean a lot to Shawna. "Check it out with your parents and see if it's okay. And if you still want me to come, e-mail me," he added with a wink.

"I will," she answered enthusiastically and then slipped into Mark's room.

After Adam went downstairs, he saw that Danielle was still speaking to her neighbor in the backyard. He waved, called, "I'll see you soon," and then went to his car. The cocktail party tonight at Dylan's was on his mind. He wasn't sure what had made him ask Leigh. Certainly not that kiss. *That* had been a monumental mistake. He'd given in to an impulse and a need that he usually kept in check.

Why she was still so attractive to him he didn't know. It had been years since she'd first rocked his world, and he wasn't about to let her rock it again. She was leaving Portland in June, and he had to keep that fact firmly in place in his head.

Asking her along tonight had simply been a practical solution to a problem. Usually he went to these parties alone. Sometimes an unattached female would latch on to him, and without an actual date along, it could be hard to extricate himself politely. He really hated the mingle-and-shake-hands parties that Dylan was so good at. Adam would rather give a presentation on new software, go over marketing strategy, analyze focus group results. However, Dylan had informed him that contacts would be at this party that could take new products global.

Having Leigh on his arm could make the night easier.

When Leigh opened her apartment door to Adam that evening, he had to take a deep breath. She looked more beautiful than he'd ever seen her. Her blond hair was arranged in loose curls on the top of her head. The strapless pink cocktail dress had a sequined bodice and a short, straight skirt. Every one of her curves was evident. The only remnant of the girl she once had been were those big blue eyes.

She smiled almost shyly. "Is this appropriate? I wasn't sure what to wear. I just bought it this morning."

"You didn't have to buy a new dress."

"I don't go to many cocktail parties."

He thought about the prom they hadn't attended. Neither of them had been able to afford it. Instead they had eaten at a fast-food restaurant and gone to a movie. Neither of them had minded then...at least *he* hadn't.

She was gazing at the pintucks on his white starched shirt, and a small smile slipped across her lips.

"What?" he asked.

"You look comfortable in that tux. As if you were born to it."

"I consider it a uniform on nights like these. Believe me, I'll be glad to get rid of the tie at the end of the evening."

Motioning inside, Leigh asked, "Would you like to come in for a few minutes?"

"I don't want to intrude on your mom's evening."

"She's not here. She went to the mall with a friend."

With Leigh looking the way she did tonight, he knew it wasn't a good idea to be alone with her. Glancing at his watch, he decided, "We'd better get going or Dylan will be ringing my cell phone."

Leigh lifted her small purse. "I have mine along just in case we get the results of your test. It's early yet, I know. But we can hope."

"I saw Mark today. It wasn't one of his better days."

"I'm sorry to hear that." She was quiet for a moment, then said, "I'm going to be taking a bunch of kids who've been in cancer treatment to the zoo tomorrow. Why don't you come along? It might help to hear the parents' stories and see how well the kids are doing. You also might get a better handle on what Mark's going to go through. Having Marietta tell you is one thing. Actually seeing the kids who've been through it is another. Being with them always gives me a lift. They're such fighters...such survivors."

As if realizing how passionate she'd become about it, she stopped, then added quietly, "We're meeting at the entrance to the zoo at two if you're interested."

"It sounds like a good idea. I met Shawna, Mark's sister, today. She seems like a great kid, too, but she's definitely worried about her brother."

"Why don't I give Shawna and Chad a call in the morning and see if they'd like to come, too?"

"Why don't you do it right now?"

"I thought we had to get to the party."

"This is more important. If Dylan calls, I'll tell him we're on our way."

In Leigh's apartment Adam felt like a bull in a china shop. Everything was so feminine, so delicate, so in place. Also, there was a funny smell in the apartment tonight—like burned...something. Yet it didn't seem to come from Leigh's kitchen area.

He listened while she made the call, and when she got off the phone, she was smiling. "I got hold of Shawna. She said she loves the zoo and wants to come. But she thinks Chad might have plans. She said her father would drop her off, and I told her I'd take her home."

It was best if they went separately tomorrow, Adam supposed. After all, he and Leigh weren't dating.

After Leigh stepped away from the phone, she headed for the living room. "I'm going to crack a window while we're gone. Our neighbor, Mr. Benson, puts supper on the stove and then forgets it's there while he's watching TV. I think Mom said he burned lima beans tonight."

Leigh's shawl, lying over the chair, didn't look warm enough for the cold, damp night. But he knew women often dressed for effect rather than warmth. As she went to the window, she looked so delectably feminine. Unlocking it, she tried to raise it, but apparently it was stuck.

"The landlord painted a few weeks ago," she explained.

Coming up behind her, Adam offered, "Let me try."

The skin of Leigh's shoulders was a creamy temptation as he stood next to her looking down at her. She'd worn a single pearl necklace and tiny pearls at her ears. His fingers itched to brush the skin along her jawline, itched to feel her soft cheek. That kiss had reminded him too much of how they'd been together, how they could be together again. He dismissed that thought as foolhardy.

With his fist, he pounded along the sash, then took hold of the lever and pulled up the window. "A few inches enough?" he asked.

When he glanced at her, she was watching him. He felt that tingling sexual tension he'd never been able to deny between them.

"A few inches is fine." Her voice was low. "It might start raining again."

"Will your mother be back soon?"

"Anytime."

They were making small talk, having a conversation that had nothing to do with the tension in the air, the thoughts they were both having—thoughts that would *not* become reality.

Stepping away from the window and Leigh, he motioned to the door. "We'd better go."

Leigh didn't respond, just crossed the room and picked up her shawl. When she laid it over her arm absently, Adam advised, "You'd better put that on. Warmer weather's supposed to move in but it hasn't yet."

As she unfolded the black velvet, he took it from her. Maybe he was torturing himself, but it was only for tonight. Her scent was so damn sweet, her lips such a pretty pink, her whole look so feminine. His fingers brushed the stray hair at the nape of her neck that had escaped the topknot. As he settled the shawl over her shoulders, he wanted to surround her with his arms the way the material was doing. He wanted to turn her around, kiss her and take her to the bedroom.

But they didn't even know each other anymore. He never went to bed with a woman simply for the sex. It had to be more than that. Even when he thought there was more, the women he'd been involved with the past few years hadn't interested him for more than a couple of months. He wasn't sure what long-lasting, committed relationships were all about. His adoptive father and mother had been together until his father's death, but Adam didn't think they'd ever been really happy.

Picturing Jared and Danielle Cambry, he'd detected silent communication between the two of them and a bond that was strong. How did a man find that?

When Leigh took the shawl from his hands, he released it, as well as thoughts of what he wanted to do with her. As they went to the door, he decided tonight was going to be about business, and Leigh would be the buffer he needed to make it all the more tolerable.

Twenty minutes later Leigh was still trembling inside as Adam escorted her into Dylan's condo. It was a penthouse apartment with windows everywhere. Still, the chrome and smoked glass, the bar with its bartender in the living room, tuxedoed waiters carrying trays of champagne and hors d'oeuvres didn't make the impression they should have. Even the original oil paintings on the walls couldn't snag her attention. All she could do was relive those moments with Adam in her apartment as they'd stood at the window.

Electricity had seemed to spark around them. Then when he'd helped her with her shawl and his fingers had brushed her neck...

The memory of that touch remained just as other memories did. Adam was so controlled, so guarded sometimes. What more could she expect?

He'd cared about her. She had betrayed those feelings by walking away. In June she'd be walking away again. He was right to keep himself removed, and she should do the same.

He will probably come to the zoo tomorrow. However Shawna would be there and so would a crowd of other people.

As Leigh glanced around, she saw there was certainly a crowd here tonight—women in sequined and beaded dresses, both long and short, men mostly wearing tuxedos. Everyone seemed to know one another.

Inside the door, a maid took Leigh's wrap. "Do you think I'll be able to find it again?" she asked Adam as the maid walked away.

"When you're ready to leave, Patrice will appear with it as if out of nowhere. Dylan always asks for her because she's good."

"You mean he doesn't have a maid all the time?"

Adam laughed. "Not Patrice, anyway. He has a housekeeper, Mrs. Warren, who cleans, does laundry and makes sure everything stays straightened up. She's a great cook, too."

"Would you like to have a housekeeper?"

"No, thanks. I have a cleaning lady who comes in once a week and a laundry service for the things I can't wash and dry myself. I like my solitude. Dylan enjoys being waited on hand and foot, but I don't.

"Speaking of the devil..." Adam drawled with a grin as Dylan strode toward them.

"Nice to see you again, Leigh."

"You, too," she said sincerely. Something about Dylan was ingratiating. He was the boy-next-door type of friendly that was comfortable.

"I hope you enjoy yourself tonight," he said with an easy smile.

"I'm sure I will. This is a beautiful apartment."

"She's especially impressed by Patrice," Adam joked.

"Uh-oh. I think Adam's telling tales about me again. I do know how to throw a party without a maid and bartender, but it's much easier to do it with them. And since Adam has made me a rich man—"

"You're my partner," Adam cut in. "We do the work together."

"Yes, but you could have done it on your own. I don't know if I would have the vision and the discipline without you." He focused his attention on her again. "Anyway, before Adam contradicts everything I've said, let me get you a glass of champagne. Why don't you come with me, and I'll introduce you to some people.''

''You don't think I can do that?'' Adam asked with a half smile.

''I'm sure you can. But I think it's best if you go over there and talk to Gregory Treporri. He's been itching to meet you, and he can do us a lot of good.''

Adam glanced over at the gray-haired man in his sixties. ''Do you mind?'' he asked Leigh.

She could tell he didn't want her to feel adrift. ''No, go ahead. I'm always eager to meet new people. This should be fun.''

After Dylan introduced Leigh to a group of men and women, one conversation developed into another. She listened to a banker discuss the world's economy, a real estate agent expound on the best deals in Portland and a model describe every detail at a shoot she'd just finished. Looking around every now and then for Adam, Leigh noticed a pretty redhead approach him as he finished his conversation with the first gentleman.

The redhead was much taller than Leigh, much leggier, and had a look of perfection about her. She wore a little black dress that hugged every curve. Leigh attempted to keep her mind on a university professor's remarks about California's next earthquake, but she couldn't help being interested in what was happening with Adam. After the discussion in Leigh's circle ebbed, she went to the bar for an orange juice, then nibbled at the buffet table. She felt out of her element here, and she was. Not that she couldn't intelligently engage in conversation, but she wasn't connecting on a personal level and that was unusual.

Adam was still talking with the beautiful redhead when he caught her eye and motioned to her. Not hesitating for a second, she joined him.

When Leigh stood next to Adam, he surprised her by circling her waist with his arm, his hand distractingly settling on her hip. He nodded to the redhead. "Leigh Peters, meet Nicole Jackson. Nicole, this is Leigh."

From Adam's body language, his possessive arm around Leigh's waist, it was obvious he was telling Nicole that Leigh was his date tonight.

Nicole's smile wasn't quite so bright now as she managed a hello. She asked Leigh, "Are you new in town?"

"Oh, no. I've lived here since I was seventeen."

"Leigh and I met in high school," Adam explained, making it sound as if they'd been together for a very long time.

"I see. Usually Adam doesn't bring a date to Dylan's parties." Nicole was apparently fishing for more information.

"Usually I don't stay at Dylan's parties very long," Adam said.

Suddenly Leigh realized exactly what was going on. Adam wanted to extricate himself from this woman's interest and he was using *her*. He was intimating they were involved when they weren't. Anger bubbled up; Leigh didn't like the idea of being used as a smokescreen.

Pulling away from Adam's hold, she gave Nicole a

very bright smile. "I just saw Dylan go into the kitchen. Will you excuse me? There was something I wanted to ask him about his decorator."

Before either Adam or Nicole could comment, she was wending through the guests on the way to the kitchen. She had seen Dylan go in there, but right now she just wanted an escape.

However, she'd only just stepped into the gleaming black and tan kitchen when she found Adam beside her, his hand on her arm. "Leigh, are you all right?"

Dylan had turned at the sound of Adam's voice. He'd been looking for something in the refrigerator.

Now he asked, "Is something wrong?"

Holding on to her temper, Leigh managed, "Everything's just fine. You're giving a beautiful party, Dylan."

With a puzzled look, Dylan glanced at Adam and then back at Leigh. "Would you two like some privacy?"

Leigh said, "No" at the same time Adam said, "Yes."

Dylan chuckled and then drawled, "O—kay. I just came in here to look for olives. The bartender said we ran out. But I can do that later." As he left the kitchen, he told Adam, "I'll head off anyone who tries to come in."

Leigh quickly started after Dylan. "There's no need for that. In fact, if you just tell me where the powder room is located—"

This time Adam firmly clasped her arm and didn't let go. "*I'll* show you where the powder room is after we talk."

Wisely Dylan slipped out of the room.

Leigh looked up at Adam. "I don't think we have anything to talk about."

His deep voice was concerned. "What's gotten you so ruffled?"

"I don't like being used. I thought you invited me here tonight because we'd...mended fences and could become friends again. But that wasn't the reason, was it?"

Adam's face had set into an unreadable mask. "No, that's not the reason. I thought you'd make the evening more pleasant."

"Pleasant?"

He shrugged. "I needed a date, Leigh. It was better to come with someone I knew. I could more easily extricate myself from a situation I didn't like—whether it's from a windy investment banker or an account manager from a cosmetics company."

"And you didn't consider how I'd feel?"

"I thought you'd enjoy mingling...that you'd have a good time."

"Did you really? Or was this some kind of payback?"

An emotion flickered in Adam's eyes, but she couldn't tell what it was. Surprise that she'd figured it out?

"I'm not stupid, Adam. You were hurt all those years ago. I'm sorry about that, but can't you see we were too young for whatever was happening between us?"

"We *were* young, Leigh. You left and I got over it. Tonight has nothing to do with that. I look at the world in realistic terms now. Bringing you here tonight was simply practical. I didn't have an ulterior motive."

Adam had always been honest with her. Yet on the other hand, he'd always been able to deny what was going on inside of him, too.

After he studied her for a few silent moments, he finally admitted, "Okay, I understand now. No one likes to feel used."

She suddenly saw that must have been the way he'd felt ten years ago. After he'd taken her under his wing and made her feel at home in Portland, she'd left his life.

"Would you like to leave?" he asked.

Being with him now was going to be uncomfortable. Since she finally knew the score, though, she wouldn't be distracted by him and could maybe dive into the party with a little more enthusiasm.

"We can stay. But I'm not going to hang on your arm like an ornament. I don't do that, Adam."

Could she see a smile in his eyes? Did she see respect there? She couldn't really tell. So she turned away and she went back out into the dining room, determined to have fun if it killed her.

Chapter Six

As Adam started across the street to the entrance of the Oregon Zoo, he spotted Leigh immediately. He'd not been here often, even though it was only five minutes from downtown Portland. He'd brought a date to the summer concert series a few years back. That woman had come and gone, and he hadn't thought much about the zoo after that....

Until Leigh suggested he come today. Adam wasn't sure what Leigh's attitude would be. She was standing in front of one of the ticket booths with children and parents. Last night, her upset with him had surprised him. He'd asked her to Dylan's party for practical reasons. Yet she'd obviously read more into it than that. They hadn't been together much after their talk in Dylan's kitchen, and she'd been quiet on the way home.

He didn't know what she expected from him.

After all, they were strangers now, even though they'd known each other long ago. Their meeting up again had been sheer chance. If she weren't on a determined course toward something much bigger, maybe he'd let old feelings rise again. But she *was* still on a determined course. That kiss at his ranch had shown him he was better off keeping his distance. He didn't *want* to want her again.

As Adam started up the incline, he could see at least five children gathered around Leigh—two were bald, one had a bandanna covering her head, another sported an inch of new hair growth spiking over his scalp. They all wore smiles and gathered close to Leigh's sides as if she were a pied piper.

The smell of French fries and grilled hamburgers wafted to the entrance from a nearby restaurant. Adam stopped halfway up the incline, watching as Leigh smiled at the kids, hugged one, dropped an arm around another's shoulder. She was dressed in a more relaxed fashion today with jeans and light blue hooded jacket. At this time of year rain was always a possibility.

One of the parents—a tall, lean brunette—approached Leigh with a smile.

As Adam walked toward them, he heard the woman say, "We can't thank you enough for all the care you gave Marcy when she was in the hospital. She still talks about how nice you were, how you read her a book one night when she couldn't get to sleep. You make a difference, Miss Peters. I hope you know that."

Leigh looked embarrassed and her cheeks flushed.

"I love working with children because they're so appreciative of everything I do. Sometimes they seem so lost in those hospital beds, and I just want to make them feel as if they're not alone."

"You did that for Marcy when we couldn't be with her. She couldn't wait to come today."

Silently Adam stood unmoving until the woman bustled her daughter into the entrance line.

Leigh's gaze came up to meet his as he joined her. Her smile dimmed a bit, and he found he didn't like that. He didn't like that at all. Still, he had to remind himself this wasn't a date. He'd come to be around the kids, hoping they could help him relate to Mark.

"I didn't think you'd come," Leigh said honestly.

"Why not?"

"Mark's not a large part of your life. You don't even know if you're a match yet."

"No, I don't. But even if I'm not a match, I plan to stay in touch with Mark. And if I'm not a match, I'd like to do everything I can to *find* him a match."

When Leigh examined his face, Adam felt as if she saw too much. She knew how unhappy he'd been growing up with his adoptive family. Maybe it was wishful thinking on his part to believe the Cambrys would accept him as family. But right now Mark was all that mattered.

Someone called to Leigh. Adam saw Shawna running toward them, a wide smile on her face.

"Hi! Sorry if I'm late. Dad dropped me off on his way to a meeting in town. I was playing chess with Mark and tried to convince him to eat lunch."

"Did the convincing do any good?" Adam asked.

"Some. Our housekeeper made him some chicken soup yesterday, and he actually ate most of the bowl." Shawna looked at the kids who were milling about. "Are we ready?"

"We're more than ready," Leigh answered. "Come on, let me introduce you to everyone."

The kids obviously loved the zoo. They chattered and pointed and giggled at the first exhibit of mountain goats cavorting on a rocky hill. Several of them pinched their noses shut when they walked down the curved ramp leading to the circular penguin house. They soon forgot the smell as they watched through the knee-to-ceiling window as penguins toddled around on a lifelike iceberg.

The awed expressions on the kids' faces were unmatchable as they entered the polar bears' "ice cave" with its dim blue lighting. Adam wasn't a camera buff but he wished he'd brought one. He saw that many of the parents had theirs. After they stepped outside once again, at their request, he took lots of pictures of the parents with their kids.

When Leigh came up to Adam after he'd taken a few at the elephant exhibit at the far end of the zoo, she gave him one of the smiles he loved. Then she said, "You're helping them keep a picture of a memory forever."

There was a viewing area for the elephants under an arbor. One of the parents slipped a quarter into the magnifying machine for her son. Adam understood that every memory was important to these parents—every smile, every burst of laughter, every wide-eyed look of surprise. He could see now why Leigh had wanted him to come along. Shawna was just as involved with the kids as he was. He watched while she lifted one little boy so he could use the magnifier.

At one point, Shawna walked beside Adam sipping her soda. "I told Mom and Dad I wanted you at my birthday party. They said you're welcome to come and bring a guest. Lissa and Sullivan are supposed to be back. Maybe you can meet your twin for the first time at our place."

Meeting his sister...his twin. It was hard to wrap his mind around the idea.

"I'll be there," he assured Shawna. "I don't know about bringing a guest."

She shrugged. "Whatever. Just so *you're* there." With a nonchalance only a teenager could possess, she added, "So you know, I invited Leigh, too."

Then she gave him a little-sister smile that, in spite of his turmoil about Leigh, made him grin back in return. It was nice knowing Shawna wanted him at the party. It was nice knowing Mark enjoyed his e-mail. Growing up, he'd told himself he didn't need connections, but now the beginning bonds forming with Mark and Shawna felt right.

Most of the group was standing at a concession stand that sold souvenirs. A handsome man who looked to be around forty saw Leigh, called to her and came over and gave her a hug. Adam found himself much too interested in the scene. The newcomer was dressed much as Adam was in jeans, athletic shoes, and a leather jacket. Adam couldn't hear what the man and Leigh were saying, but they were laughing a lot in between the conversational bits. The guy even took

Leigh's hand once and gave it a squeeze, and before he left, gave her another hug and a kiss on the cheek.

Adam felt a knot in his gut and was glad when the group started moving again. A short time later he saw that Leigh was standing alone.

Hands in his jacket pockets, he walked up beside her. "I think they're getting worn-out," he commented. A few of the kids were dragging now, yet they still were having a good time and didn't seem to want to go home.

"They're not the only ones."

She didn't look as if she were dragging, not at all, but she did look a bit distracted. Did it have something to do with that man?

Adam nodded in the direction from which they'd come. "Was that guy back there an old friend?"

She looked surprised he'd brought it up. "Sort of."

When she didn't say more, Adam pressed, "Or is he an old flame?"

"Reed and I met at a workshop a couple of years ago. We dated for a while."

"He's a doctor?"

"He's a psychologist. I liked him a lot, but he was ready to get married, settle down and have kids. I still had too many things I wanted to accomplish. I haven't gotten involved with anyone for that reason."

"You certainly are single-minded." In a way Adam admired that, but in another way… "Leigh, you know being a doctor isn't going to fulfill your every need. Don't you want more than that?"

"After I earn my medical degree, I can *have* more than that. I've known women who had to drop out of school because they couldn't balance work and a family.''

''There should be a happy medium.''

''Have you found a happy medium, Adam? From what I've seen of your life, work fills it up. You don't seem to have any committed relationships, either.''

''Maybe that's because I've decided getting involved demands too high a price if it doesn't work out.''

They gazed at each other then, lost in what could have been.

They might have stood there that way forever, silent, separate, thinking about what had happened ten years before, except for the fact that Shawna came running over to them, all excited as only a fifteen-almost-sixteen-year-old could be. ''Mrs. Bristol, Tommy's mom, asked me if I'm free to baby-sit. She likes the way I've been relating to Tommy. Isn't that great?''

Refocusing his attention on Shawna, Adam broke eye contact with Leigh. ''Do you baby-sit often?''

She shook her head. ''Only with Mark. I told her she could call Mom, and Mom would tell her how responsible I am. I'm thinking about being a teacher because I like being with kids. If I do a really good job, maybe Mrs. Bristol will spread the word and I'll get lots of practice.''

Even with the tension zipping back and forth between him and Leigh, Adam couldn't help but admire this teenager. She was everything he'd ever want a daughter of his own to be.

A daughter of his own. Since when had he thought about having kids?

Shawna gave both him and Leigh a quick appraisal. "Is something wrong?"

Leigh's smile was forced. "No, nothing's wrong. I think this excursion has just tired out all of us."

"Yeah, the parents are talking about taking their kids home. Are we leaving, too?"

"That's probably a good idea. Why don't we go over and say goodbye to everybody."

Shawna looked at Adam. "Are you leaving?"

"Yes, I'm going back to my office for a while. Tell Mark to look for an e-mail tonight. I took some pictures of Thunder. I'll download them and send them to him."

"He'll like that," Shawna said with a smile. "Don't forget to put my birthday party on your calendar."

"I won't forget."

When Leigh turned to go, Adam wanted to clasp her shoulder, keep her there, straighten things out between them. But pride kept him still, kept his hands at his sides, kept his guard up.

"Goodbye, Leigh," he said in a low voice.

"Goodbye, Adam," she returned with a bit of sadness.

Then she was walking away, and he stood there alone.

For the past three days, Leigh had tried to think of everything and anything except for Adam. It wasn't quite so difficult when she was working. She'd accepted a double shift yesterday because she simply couldn't keep analyzing what Adam had meant to her and what he could mean to her again.

Actually that wasn't true. He obviously hadn't forgotten and hadn't forgiven her for what had happened ten years ago. How could she blame him? If their positions had been reversed…

Unfortunately, tonight her mother was working late, and Leigh had no distraction at all as she came home, made herself a supper of a tuna salad sandwich, carrot sticks and rice pudding her mom had bought at the deli. After that she thought about her options. She could go out somewhere and try to keep herself distracted, but she'd already shopped for groceries on Monday and had no desire to walk the mall or even go ice-skating. Her other option was to stay in and do something productive—like cleaning. Then her mother wouldn't have to give up the little spare time she had to do it. Decision made, Leigh put her few dishes in the dishwasher, changed into navy leggings and a red T-shirt, then tugged the vacuum cleaner from the pantry closet.

It was almost seven o'clock by the time she finished vacuuming. She was thinking about taking down the curtains and shaking them out outside when the doorbell rang.

Leigh smiled. It was probably Mr. Benson. Often he came over to borrow an egg or a cup of sugar, or to ask to borrow their broom. She guessed he really didn't need anything he borrowed, but rather that he was lonely and he wanted someone to talk to. Leigh always asked questions of the elderly widower—how his son was doing, what new feat his granddaughter had accomplished, when his family would be visiting him next. Tonight she was glad for any interruption that would fill up her time as she quickly went to the door.

However, when she opened it, she didn't find Mr. Benson. She found Adam.

Knowing she looked a mess—strands of hair had escaped her ponytail while she was working—she felt heat flush her cheeks. Unable to contain her surprise, she asked, "What are you doing here?"

He was wearing a blue-and-black rugby shirt and black jeans. His expression betrayed nothing as he asked, "May I come in?"

Not only she was a mess, but the apartment was a mess. She'd moved the furniture to sweep, vacuum cleaner attachments lay here and there, and small throw rugs were draped over the armchair. Recalling their "nondate" Saturday night and the tension between them on Sunday, she replied, "This isn't a good time."

Adam didn't seem put off by her reluctance to let him in. "Is your mother home?"

"No, she's not."

"Then this *is* a good time, Leigh. We need to talk."

It had rained again today and was still raining now. Adam's hair was damp and there were drops of rain on his shirt. He smelled male and damp and sexy. The look in his eyes was so intensely encompassing that all she could do was back up a few steps and watch him enter the apartment.

The chaos inside seemed to surprise him.

"I'm cleaning." It was a lame explanation, but all she could offer for the moment.

"I can see that." However, the chaos didn't deter him, and he went over to the sofa and waited for her to join him.

After she perched near the arm, he lowered himself to the middle, his gaze on her all the while. "I thought about what you said Saturday night—that I'd asked you along to use you…for a payback. I didn't believe that was my intent, but after what came out of my mouth at the zoo, I realized maybe it was. I thought we had *more* than a teenage crush. You were more than a new girl in town who I dated for a while. I had started weaving dreams about us, Leigh. I thought you had started dreaming, too."

"I had," she admitted. "But Mom reminded me my other dreams were important, too."

"You obviously didn't think we could work on dreams together. You didn't have any faith in what was happening between us."

Walking away from Adam had hurt her, but now she realized how all of it had looked to him. "Can we get past what happened?" she asked now.

"I'm not sure there's any point in getting past it. This summer you'll be leaving for Cleveland. But I had no right to say what I did yesterday. I have no right to judge your life. You've set your goals and I admire them. Believe me, I understand about wanting to succeed, about reaching for something more than you had. In your case, you're reaching for both you and your mother."

Adam was on target with that. She certainly

couldn't deny it. "So where do we go from here?" she almost whispered.

He moved toward her then, and her heart pounded so hard she could hardly catch her breath.

"Where do you *want* to go from here?"

"I don't know. I just know I want you to forgive me. I didn't want to hurt you. I—" She couldn't help the quick tears that came to her eyes and caused a large lump in her throat.

When Adam reached toward her, Leigh closed her eyes. She felt him finger a strand of hair along her cheek. Her body trembled as he brushed a few more behind her ear. Then he wiped away one small tear that had escaped from under her lashes.

"Leigh," he said hoarsely.

Adam's kisses had always made her world spin, and now as his palm caressed her cheek, as his lips covered hers, the light and excitement and fire racing inside of her brought alive needs that had been asleep. It wasn't long before his tongue slipped into her mouth.

She reached for him, wanting to relive experiences they'd shared, wanting to touch him again. When she caressed the back of his neck, he groaned. She could feel the same tension in his body that was coiling inside of her. His tongue coaxed hers into a mating that was intimate, seductive and thoroughly arousing. After he pulled the scrunchie from her ponytail, he ran his fingers through her hair, angled her head and ravished her more completely. Although Adam's passion had always been hotly intense, he was incredibly tender, too. That's what made it so overwhelming. That's what made her lose herself in him.

When his mouth broke away from hers, she thought he was going to stop. She knew it was best if he *did* stop. But Adam apparently had no intention of ending what they had started. His lips trailed soft, wet kisses down her throat. One of his hands stroked her midriff, then moved higher to caress her breast. She was being swept away into an erotic watershed of desire.

Mindlessly she arched into his hand, wanting to feel more, do more. But he was in control. He was leading her, and she could only follow.

As his hand left her breast, she opened her eyes and she could see the fierce need in his. Without a word he lifted her shirt up and over her head, then he unhooked her bra. When she made no move to stop him, he cupped her breast in his hand and fingered the nipple, all the while never moving his gaze from hers. She should be blushing. She should be embarrassed. She should be trying to clear her head of the sexual haze to make sense of what was happening. But Adam was filling her world, not leaving any space for anything else, as he took both of her breasts into his hands and thumbed the nipples simultaneously. She felt as if rockets were going off inside of her. With deliberate slowness, he made incredibly slow rotations around her breasts and passed his hands down her sides. His thumbs met at her navel, and they traced her rib cage.

She could hardly sit still. As arousal cloaked Leigh in its excitement, Adam bent his head to her breast. The chaos in the room and in her heart and in her head vanished in an awareness of only him. His lips were masterful as they teased and taunted her and she breathed his name. After he stopped for only a second, he leaned back on the sofa taking her with him, stretching his legs out under her. She realized Adam had gotten terrifically experienced at foreplay, though she didn't know if she could stand much more. His hands slid over her backside, and the stretchy material of her leggings seemed to be no barrier at all. She could feel every stroke as if she were naked. Her breasts pressed against the cotton of his shirt and she could feel each one of his breaths. Most of all, she was aware of his powerful arousal. The heavy denim of his jeans couldn't hide it and she melted over him, wanting to feel more of it.

He brought his arms around her and kissed her again. It was a hungry kiss, marking everything she could give. When she responded with the same hunger, his hands slid up her shoulders into her hair.

Breaking it off, he growled, "I want you."

"I want you, too," she whispered.

Taking her at her word, he hooked his thumbs in her leggings and started to drag them down. She wiggled and slid and helped any way she could until they were around her ankles. Using her feet to kick them off, she started on the buttons on Adam's shirt. They were both breathing hard. They were both in a hurry to get them undressed. They were both aware of an urgency that defied reason.

"I have to sit up to get my shirt off," Adam muttered. Then he gave her a wry grin. "But I don't want to stop this."

"I'll be able to touch you a lot better if your shirt's off."

Her honest words brought a flair of desire to his

eyes, and moments later he was bare-chested and her fingers were sifting through thick brown hair. She looked up and then found herself lost in another kiss.

The phone rang.

Adam didn't break away and Leigh didn't care. She had an answering machine.

His tongue suggestively stroked hers.

The phone rang again.

Neither of them paid it any heed…neither of them cared who was calling.

However, after the fourth ring, a deep male voice said, "Leigh, it's Dr. Chambers. I'll leave a message here, then I'll also try to reach you on your cell phone."

Adam and Leigh broke apart at the same moment. Leigh was on her feet racing to the kitchen as Dr. Chambers went on, "The results of the tests are back."

Her breath coming in short gasps, she plucked the receiver from its cradle and somehow managed to find her voice. "Dr. Chambers? It's Leigh."

"Leigh. Wonderful. I'm so glad you're there. I know you want to give this information to Mr. Bartlett as soon as you can. He's a perfect match."

Adam had followed Leigh to the phone. As she took in the news, she sent up a prayer of thanks. Mark had a chance now, he really did—that is if Adam went through with the harvesting procedure. With the way he felt about hospitals—

"I'll tell Adam…Mr. Bartlett. What about the Cambrys?"

"Officially you can't say anything to them until

Bartlett signs a consent form. That's procedure, Leigh."

She knew that. She just thought that in this case since everyone knew each other… "All right. I'll tell Mr. Bartlett that, too."

"Fine. Call me back after you reach him. The faster he makes his decision, the better for Mark. If he's going to do this, we need to get the boy into the hospital and get him prepped. This is going to be a rough road for Mark, but at least he has a road now. I'll let you go so you can call Bartlett."

"Thanks, Dr. Chambers. I'll get back to you as soon as I can."

Although she was self-conscious about her nakedness now, she didn't want to keep the news from Adam any longer than she had to. "You're a perfect match. The news couldn't be any better than that. Now you have to decide if you're going to go through the harvesting procedure. The sooner you decide, the better it will be for Mark."

As Adam digested what she'd told him, she hurried to the sofa, slipped on her bra and slid into her panties and leggings, pulling them up quickly. After she tugged on her T-shirt, she joined Adam in the kitchen once again. "Do you want me to go over everything that will happen?"

She was trying to be professional when all she could do was stare at his bare chest and think about the way he had kissed her, the way he had touched her, the way she had responded with an abandon she'd never felt before. Yet another part of her was relieved the phone had rung. Making love to Adam shouldn't happen on impulse. Not with their history...not unless they were both sure they wouldn't have regrets afterward.

Adam had been staring out the kitchen window. Now he shifted and met her gaze. "Marietta explained it all thoroughly. Since I already had a physical, they'll admit me when Mark is ready for the transplant, prep me and give me anesthesia. Then they'll extract the bone marrow. I'll stay overnight and be discharged in the morning."

Her heart racing, she nodded. "Your hips will be sore, and you'll feel as if you took a bad fall on the ice. Somebody should drive you home. Have you made up your mind you want to do this?"

"I don't have any choice. I couldn't live with myself if I didn't try to save Mark's life. Can we tell him the news?"

"No one can tell him until you sign the consent papers. That's the procedure."

"All right. Fine. Then let's sign the consent papers."

Leigh checked her watch. "It's almost eight. Nobody will be at the hospital—"

"Didn't you say the sooner we do all this, the better for Mark?"

"Yes, I did." She thought about it. "Let me call Dr. Chambers back. If you sign the papers tonight, we could admit Mark in the morning."

Moments later, her conversation with the chief of staff was short and to the point. The administrator agreed to meet them at the hospital in the conference room she'd used before. He would have everything he needed with him.

When Leigh put down the phone, she looked up at Adam. He was standing a good two feet away.

"Dr. Chambers said he'd meet us there. You can sign the forms tonight."

"Good. Then we can tell the Cambrys. Are you ready?"

The sparks in Adam's eyes told her he was looking at her as if he remembered what state she'd been in just fifteen minutes before. She remembered, too. The problem was, though, he wasn't *acting* as if they'd almost made love on the sofa. He was acting as if nothing had happened.

For now, they'd have to forget about the two of them and concentrate on Mark. Maybe that's what Adam was doing and that was the distance she felt between them.

"Give me two minutes. I just want to change my T-shirt and grab a jacket."

As she hurried to the bedroom, she saw Adam move toward the window again. He stared out unseeingly, and she wished she knew what was going through his head.

Chapter Seven

Shifting gears from almost having sex with a woman to the realization that he was going to become a transplant donor kept Adam from dwelling on either for too long. Although the phone call had seemed to come at an inopportune moment, he was thankful for it now. Leigh's vulnerability had grabbed him in the gut. Impulse and an overstimulated libido had taken over. Frustratingly, he'd wanted her as he had years ago, and he'd acted on that.

However, if he'd given in to fulfilling his physical needs, he would have been sorry. Everything about this situation with Leigh was unsettling. They'd been thrown together and, apparently, neither of them knew how to react to that. Still, they weren't teenagers any longer. They were adults with adult decisions to make.

He wasn't about to become involved with Leigh Peters again when she'd be leaving in June.

After he found a place in the parking garage, they walked across the catwalk to the hospital. It seemed quiet. Adam hated the idea of Mark being admitted here and everything the young boy was going to have to go through. His own part in it…

He'd handle it as he'd handled everything else in his life. He was a master at shutting down his thoughts and doing whatever he had to do. Letting himself remember what had happened to Delia and thinking about what was going to happen next wouldn't help anyone.

They took the elevator to the fourth floor, and still Leigh didn't say anything. He didn't know if she was thinking about her job or what had almost happened on her couch. She'd avoided his gaze as they'd left her apartment.

Maybe the couch was winning.

The fluorescent glitter of the overhead lights on the tile floor brought back too many memories as Adam strode quickly to the conference room. Somehow Leigh kept up. When they arrived, the door was already open and Adam spotted Dr. Chambers and Marietta waiting inside.

"Marietta," Leigh said, surprised. "I didn't expect you to be here."

The counselor shrugged and her answer encompassed both Leigh and Adam. "Dr. Chambers wanted me here in case Adam had any questions. I'll go over the consent forms with you," she added with a patient smile.

Chambers was apparently making sure all of his bases were covered with this one. The success of this whole endeavor could bring more funding to his hospital in several ways. Adam couldn't fault the good business sense in that. It was just a shame that practicing medicine had boiled down to dollars and cents.

Was that true for Leigh, too? Is that why she wanted to become a doctor? She'd told him more than once that she was happy with the work she was doing. Then again, she might be even happier with a medical degree.

Before they took seats at the conference table, Dr. Chambers shook Adam's hand. "This is a fine thing that you're doing. I wish more people would sign up with the registry and realize they could help save lives."

"It's hard to get the word out," Leigh agreed.

After the women were seated, Adam took his chair, too. He glanced at Marietta. "I hope we didn't disturb your evening. This could have waited till morning, but I want to tell Mark and his family that he has a chance."

"I understand completely. You didn't disturb my evening. I was having dinner with my cat."

Her light tone brought a smile to Adam's lips, and he relaxed a bit, realizing that had been her intent.

For the next half hour Marietta explained the consent forms as Adam signed and dated them. In a mere nine days his life had changed drastically. He knew who his biological father was now. He knew he had a twin. Connections to Mark were becoming stronger day by day.

And Leigh?

Leigh was making him need again.

When all the necessary papers were signed, explanations made and questions answered, Dr. Chambers shook Adam's hand again.

''We're going to tell Jared and his family now. That's all right?'' Adam asked.

''Yes, that's fine. Jared knows he's supposed to contact Leigh with any questions...or he can always call me. I'll get in touch with him tomorrow because we'll have to admit Mark and get the ball rolling.''

Twenty minutes later Adam and Leigh were at Jared's front door. The lawyer himself answered and, when he saw Leigh with Adam, his expression became worried. ''Do you have news?''

''Yes, we do,'' Leigh said as Adam kept silent. ''Adam is a perfect match.''

For Adam this moment meant everything. Not only could he be a donor for Mark, but Marietta had explained the test results that confirmed he was definitely Jared's son.

Without saying anything, Jared motioned them inside. He looked stunned. ''I was afraid to hope,'' he murmured. ''Please come in. I'll get Danni.''

Suddenly there was only one place Adam wanted to be—in Mark's room, telling him the news. ''Is Mark still awake?''

''Shawna's with him.'' Jared's gaze met Adam's. ''If you want to tell him, go ahead.''

When Adam reached Mark's room, the door was ajar and he pushed it open slowly. Shawna was sitting by Mark's bed reading a magazine and the little boy looked as though he were asleep.

When Shawna saw Adam, she came to the door. "He fell asleep a few minutes ago."

"I don't want to wake him. I have good news, though," he added with a smile he couldn't keep in.

"You're a match?" Shawna's voice rose.

"Yes. We just got the news tonight. I signed all the forms, and Dr. Chambers is going to call your dad tomorrow about admitting Mark and getting the conditioning started."

"I wish Chad were here so I could tell him. His way of dealing with this is to hang out with his friends. He's hardly ever home."

"Maybe now that will change."

"Maybe it will. Oh, I can't believe this!" She clasped Adam's arm. "You're really my brother."

He couldn't suppress his grin. "I guess I am."

"I feel like I've been holding my breath ever since you got tested," she admitted.

This teenager was so open, and Adam admired that. In some ways she reminded him of Leigh when Leigh had been in high school. "I feel that way, too. I want to celebrate yet I know we have a long way to go." He was warning her that they weren't out of the woods, and she was intelligent enough to get that.

"I'm going to sit here with Mark until he wakes up even if it's the middle of the night so I can tell him. I'm sure he'll want to e-mail you right away."

"I doubt if I'll get much sleep tonight. If he e-mails, I'll get right back to him."

Suddenly Shawna threw her arms around Adam and

gave him a giant hug. "Thank you. Thank you for doing this."

A tightness wound about Adam's heart and he found it hard to speak. So he didn't. He hugged her back instead.

After Shawna had returned to Mark's bedside, Adam took a deep breath and went downstairs. Hearing voices in the kitchen, he headed that way. When he saw only Danielle and Leigh sitting at the table, he felt disappointed but also relieved. There was always an awkwardness with Jared that he didn't know what to do with.

Apparently Danielle felt she had to explain. "Jared went out for a walk. This whole situation with Mark and with you has affected him deeply. He's not a man who expresses his feelings easily and I think he's just trying to get a handle on all of it. But I certainly don't want you to think he's not grateful because he is. Without you—" her voice caught "—I don't know what we would have done."

Taking a seat at the table, Adam hoped to learn more about this family. "Shawna said Chad's been out with friends a lot. I was hoping to meet him."

"You'll meet him at Shawna's birthday party on Saturday night if not before."

"You're still going to have it?" Adam asked.

"Absolutely. Mark will be in the hospital having tests run, and I'll be with him as much as I can. But I have to be here for my daughter, too. After the chemo starts, I won't be able to be by Mark's side, but I'll stay at the hospital anyway. They'll limit his contact severely...even with us."

"I understand there'll be a few days of testing for him before that starts."

"Yes."

"I'll check in on you whenever I can," Leigh assured Danielle. "We'll have specialized nurses for the transplant-conditioning process he's going through, but I'll make sure he knows I'm there, too."

"Thank you," Danielle murmured and ducked her head.

Adam could see her emotions were very close to the surface, and he wondered how his father dealt with that.

Abruptly Danielle raised her head, wiped a tear from the corner of her eye and smiled at them. "Enough about us. Adam, I want to know about you. I'm hoping Lissa will be home in time for Shawna's party. Maybe you can meet her and Sullivan then."

Maybe. Or maybe he could give his sister a call before then. "Where did she and—Sullivan is it?—go on their honeymoon?"

"Scotland. I think they're coming back Thursday or Friday. I'm sure she can't wait to hear from you. Don't hesitate to call her."

Adam wondered if his father knew what a gem he had in Danielle—she was such a positive woman.

"Mark has been telling me all about your software company and the programs you gave him," she said now. "I even tried the one with dinosaurs. It was fun."

As the discussion moved toward Adam's life, how he and Dylan had started Novel Programs, Unlimited, in college, he glanced at Leigh. She'd been extremely quiet ever since they'd left her apartment. They'd have to talk about what had happened there. They couldn't ignore it. Now that her liaison work was finished, they wouldn't have to see each other if they didn't want to. Adam knew that would probably be best.

As the hour grew later and Jared hadn't returned, Adam and Leigh said their goodbyes.

In the car Leigh turned to Adam. "I think Mr. Cambry was overwhelmed by all of it. I don't think he knew how to thank you."

"Maybe. Maybe he's not thinking about me at all. Mark's the one he's concerned about and he should be. I belong to a time in his life he probably wants to forget."

Talking to Leigh here about what had happened at her apartment didn't seem right somehow, so he waited. However, when they pulled into the apartment's parking lot, she said, "Mom's home."

Adam switched off the ignition and shifted toward her. If they wouldn't have privacy inside, they'd have to have it out here. Rain had begun falling, and it dripped down the windshield in slow rivulets. Adam knew he wasn't great at tact. Dylan was the diplomat.

"I suppose your job as liaison is over now," he commented.

"That depends on Dr. Chambers. He might want me to help keep the Cambrys informed during the transplant process. And then there's your procedure."

Adam shrugged dismissively. "I'll get admitted one day, I'll be out the next. No big deal."

Under the parking lot's lights, he saw Leigh studying him. "What?" he asked, wondering what she was thinking.

"You're a lot like your father."

"Jared?"

She nodded. "It's hard to tell what he's thinking and especially what he's feeling. You're like that, too. You always have been."

Leigh had said it matter-of-factly, but it didn't sound like a compliment. He knew he felt that Jared was shutting him out right now. Did Leigh feel he was shutting her out? Well, he *was*...with good reason.

"I only talk about what I feel is necessary to talk about," he said in a low tone.

"Do you think it's necessary to talk about what happened tonight?" she asked quietly.

He understood the conversation was all about them and had nothing to do with the Cambrys now. "Is that why you've been so quiet? You're thinking about what happened?"

She seemed to take her time answering, as if she were weighing her words. "Mark's situation is serious enough to make me quiet. But, yes, my silence has more to do with what happened with us."

She stopped as if thinking about going on. But then she blurted out, "You acted as if *nothing* happened, just as you acted after you kissed me. I guess I'm wondering if that's really true. I wondered why you came by tonight."

After a few moments of thoughtful silence, he replied, "I came by because I felt I hadn't been fair to you, and I wanted to tell you that. I didn't intend for anything else to happen."

Looking away from him then, she stared out into the black night. "But it did. Were you sorry about it?"

Even when they were teenagers, Leigh had pushed him to examine what he was feeling. Back then it didn't feel quite as uncomfortable as it did now. "It was enjoyable, Leigh."

"Enjoyable? Don't you understand, Adam, that I don't just *do* that with any man? I haven't been intimate with another man since I was intimate with *you.*"

Bombshells had been dropping all around Adam for the past week and a half. He shouldn't be surprised that another one had just smashed into his car. "Why not?"

She seemed totally exasperated that he'd asked the question. "Because you meant a lot to me and I never wanted to get involved with a man unless I felt that way again."

His hand tightened on the steering wheel. "Is that the real reason? Or is it just that you're so goal oriented that nothing else could get in the way of the career you want?"

As soon as the words were out, he saw the hurt on her face and he regretted any suspicions he'd had that she might be interested in him now because he was rich. Leigh had never been like that, and she still wasn't after money. She was after success and respect and a career to give meaning to her life.

"I can't dispute that's the impression I've given you, but it was never that simple." She turned away, stared through the windshield, then opened her door. "I'd better go in."

He didn't like the idea of her being hurt. "It's pouring again."

"I won't melt." She hopped out of the car before he could stop her.

Swearing, he decided he couldn't let her go like this. They'd probably be seeing each other at the hospital. The whole situation was tough enough without icy tension between them.

Climbing out of the car, he strode after her and caught up with her at the apartment building's door.

"Adam, there's no reason for you to come in with me." She'd put her hood up, but it had slipped down, and her hair was getting wet. She brushed it behind her ear.

He wanted to run his hands through her hair. He wanted to kiss her again. Time and place and circumstances were against them, just as they'd been long ago.

"It's late, I'll walk you up to your apartment."

Seeing the purpose in his eyes, she gave up with a resigned sigh.

As they mounted the interior stairway, their footsteps echoed against the walls.

They'd just reached her apartment door when it opened and her mother came out carrying an umbrella. "Leigh? I was worried about you. I got your note that you were at the hospital, but your car's still here. I tried to call your cell phone, but I could only get your voice mail."

"The charge probably ran out. I had it on all day in case Dr. Chambers had to get hold of me."

"Dr. Chambers? Is something wrong?"

Leigh looked to Adam and he knew she wouldn't tell her mother anything unless he gave his permission. "Leigh's been acting as liaison and has been on call for the past week or so. I was a potential donor for a transplant patient. We just found out tonight that I'm a match. I had to sign consent forms and then we went to tell the family."

Her mother was looking from one of them to the other, trying to absorb what Adam had said. "I see. So you are going to be a donor?"

"It looks that way."

"Were you matched up with the registry?"

"No. My biological father came looking for me. His son's sick and apparently I can help." It was amazing how something so big could be summed up in so few words.

"I see," Claire said again, opening the door to the apartment wider. "Would you like to come in for a cup of coffee?"

Adam didn't have to look at Leigh to know that wouldn't be advisable. Maybe this was the way it had to end. Maybe this was easier than hashing it all out, repeating what had already been said. "No. No thank you. It's time I get back to the ranch." He couldn't keep his gaze from holding Leigh's. "I imagine I'll be seeing you at the hospital."

She nodded. "Will you keep in touch with the Cambrys about what's happening with Mark, or do you want me to fill you in?"

"I'll be keeping in touch with them. I'm sure Shawna will keep me informed if Jared doesn't."

Then with a last look at the first girl he'd ever considered making vows to, he said good-night and headed for the parking lot.

After Leigh was inside the apartment, she took one look at her mother and knew they were going to have a discussion. She didn't feel like it. She'd just handed her heart to Adam and he had handed it back. No surprise there. Always guarded, he wasn't about to tell her he felt anything when she would be leaving again.

Her mother opened the closet door and put the umbrella inside. After she closed it, she shrugged out of her raincoat and hung it on a peg. "I guess that's why you didn't go into detail in your note. Confidentiality?"

Leigh hung her jacket beside her mother's raincoat. "Yes." Maybe if she kept her answers short her mother would drop the whole thing.

"It's a nice thing Adam's doing," Claire remarked offhandedly.

Going to the mug tree on the counter, Leigh took one of them and filled it with water.

"So you'll be seeing him at the hospital?" her mother prompted.

In turmoil about everything that had happened tonight, Leigh held on to her patience and set the mug inside the microwave, pressing the timer. "Yes, in conjunction with Mark's transplant."

"That's all?"

"What would you like to know, Mom?" she asked gently, deciding they might as well have this discussion now.

Her mother came around the table. "I guess I want to know if you're falling for him again."

The microwave beeped and Leigh accepted the inevitable. "I don't think I ever got over him." That had been obvious the moment she'd set eyes on him at the hospital.

"Maybe you were younger when you knew him before, but nothing's really changed. You have years of schooling ahead of you—"

"I know what I have ahead of me, Mom." She doubted if any relationship could withstand the grueling hours she'd be keeping.

"So you're not going to get involved?"

"I doubt it. But I honestly don't know."

When her mother looked troubled, Leigh couldn't reassure her, because this time the decision wasn't her mother's. It was her own. Did she want an affair with Adam for a few months? Would that be enough? Or after this evening would he shut down whatever feelings were between them?

Tonight she didn't have the answers.

When Adam returned to Cedar Run Ranch, he parked in his garage and didn't even bother changing clothes. Instead he went straight to the barn. Thunder was in his stall, although the back door that led out into the corral was open. Sometimes the big horse didn't come in but stood out in the rain or found shelter under the trees.

Adam changed into the spare clothes he kept in the tack room, then he mucked out Thunder's stall, fed the horse and left him to his meal. Picking up his clothes and shoes, Adam jogged to the house through the now sparse raindrops and let himself inside. It was quiet as it always was, but tonight it seemed too damn quiet.

Going into his home office, he dropped the clothes and shoes on a chair, then checked his e-mail. Nothing from Mark. He must still be sleeping. But the light was blinking on his answering machine and he hit Play, surprised when he heard his mother's voice.

"Adam, it's your mom. Please call me when you get in. It's important."

Important. That covered a lot of territory—from an increase in salary for the farm manager, to an illness of one of the cows, to a house problem for his mom herself. She was fifty-six now and slowing down. Life on the farm with Owen Bartlett had been tough. Then again, maybe Rena was coming home from Australia. Still...he couldn't see a family reunion in the offing. After Delia had died, it was as if his connection to the farm and the Bartletts had faded away. Owen, his mom, Sharon and Rena had become even tighter.

No point wondering about it. He made the call.

Peggy Bartlett picked up on the first ring. "Hello?"

"It's Adam. I hope it's not too late. I just got your message."

"No, it's not too late. Thank you for calling."

His mother had always been polite with him, if not warm.

"You said it was important."

"I think it is. John thinks it is. I need your help with Sharon."

Sharon was thirty-two now and still lived at home. She worked for an insurance firm in Portland but Adam didn't know much about her life. Sharon had always been the most distant from him, the most resentful that he'd been brought into the family. "What's the problem?"

"Well, uh, it isn't just Sharon. I had some news for you but it's created a problem and—"

Adam waited, letting his mother figure out what it was she wanted to tell him.

"John and I are going to get married." She said it in a rush as if she couldn't wait to get it out.

At first Adam was startled. John Pavlichek, the manager he'd hired, was in his late forties, at least seven years younger than his mother. On the other hand, he'd been living on the property for the past four years. Adam knew since Owen had died, his mother had depended heavily on John. Maybe this was a practical move on both their parts.

"Adam?"

"Yes, Mom."

"Don't you approve, either?"

"It's not up to me to approve or not approve. It's your life. I don't have a say in it."

"But you're funding John's salary. If you don't approve..."

Was she afraid he'd cut off that salary if he didn't approve? Adam paced his office and ran his hand through his hair. "That won't change, unless John has a hidden fortune and he doesn't need my salary anymore."

"He doesn't have much of his own, you know that."

Yes, Adam did know that because he'd done a complete background check on the man before he'd hired him. Pavlichek had worked as a foreman in a textile factory for twenty years. When the factory closed, he'd had trouble finding another job. He'd been working at a fast-food joint when he'd applied for the job as manager of the Bartlett farm. Adam had seen right away that John was intelligent, hardworking and just down on his luck.

"Tell John he doesn't have to worry about being out of work again."

"Thank you, Adam." There was relief in his mother's voice and he was glad to hear that at least.

"I guess congratulations are in order. When are you getting married?"

"We're not sure yet. We're just going to go to a justice of the peace and maybe out to dinner afterward. That's why I called. Sharon won't go. She insists she doesn't want anything to do with the wedding. In fact, she doesn't want John moving into the house with me. I can't make her see reason. I thought maybe you could."

"Why do you think *I'll* be able to make her see reason?"

"Because she respects what you've become even though she's never said it. I don't have anyone else to turn to, Adam. John's going to move in here whether she likes it or not. But I want...I want her blessing."

Sharon had been one of the beloved daughters. Yes, her blessing would be important. Maybe he was still trying to earn Owen Bartlett's approval after all these years, but he couldn't turn down his mother's request. "All right, I'll see what I can do. I have meetings all day tomorrow into the evening, but I can drive up on Friday. Will she be there around suppertime?''

''She should be. I'm not going to tell her you're coming. It will probably be better that way.''

A surprise attack would definitely be better. If Sharon knew he was coming, she might decide not to be there. ''Play it however you think you should. I'll be there Friday around five.''

''We'll see you then, Adam.''

He heard gratitude again in his mother's voice. He was satisfied with that.

As he went to the kitchen to finally make himself something to eat, it wasn't the visit to the farm Friday that was on his mind. For the moment it wasn't even the thought of the transplant and the procedure he'd have to go through to help Mark. Rather, Leigh was on his mind. Whenever he remembered kissing her, undressing her, his blood heated all over again. Most of all he remembered the hurt look on her face in the car. He remembered her saying, ''I haven't been intimate with another man since I was intimate with you.''

And he wondered how in the hell he was going to put her out of his head.

Chapter Eight

At 2:00 a.m., when Leigh checked the clock for at least the twentieth time, she knew falling asleep was hopeless. Pushing herself up and sliding her feet over the side of the bed, she went to her closet and reached for the string on the light inside. When she yanked it, she blinked against the glare. It was about time she admitted to herself that her feelings for Adam Bartlett had never faded.

Pulling a small step stool from the corner of the closet, she wedged it between her shoes, then stepped onto it so she could reach the back of the top shelf. It seemed everything was stacked on that shelf—from tax returns to a cosmetics case for traveling to a straw hat she wore at the beach. She remembered exactly where the box was that she was looking for. It was in the back left corner, hidden by the teddy bear that had sat in the middle of her bed when she was a little girl. The box was blue, deceiving in its sturdiness. It looked as if it could have held school reports, research notes or stationery of some kind. But it didn't hold any of those things.

With care, she slid it forward, pushing off the stack of magazines on top of it, lifted it from the shelf and took it over to her bed. After she turned on the bedside lamp, she opened it as if it held the secrets to the universe. Actually, it didn't hold any secrets, just memories.

The first memento she saw was a paper napkin from the fast-food restaurant she and Adam had enjoyed most. On it was a note he had written to her and left in her locker. "Leigh—Meet me under the bleachers after school. A."

Just like the supply closet in the school, the space under those bleachers had allowed them to have some privacy, a place to hold each other, a place to kiss.

Beside the note Leigh found three pressed red rosebuds. Adam had given her those the night of their graduation. In addition, within an envelope, she pulled out a photo taken in one of the machines in the mall as well as movie ticket stubs. She'd scrawled on each the name of the movie they'd seen.

Finally she spotted what she'd really been looking for. It was a leather bracelet with her name and Adam's branded into the rawhide. They'd gone to a street fair together and there had been lots of tables with crafts. An old man had made the bracelet and then personalized it while they waited. After Adam had bought the bracelet for her, he'd snapped it on to her wrist, and she had known exactly what that had meant. He was claiming her. He didn't want her to date anyone else and she hadn't. She hadn't even thought about dating anyone else.

Curious to see if the bracelet still fit, Leigh snapped it on to her wrist. Tracing her finger over Adam's name, she felt tears come to her eyes. She'd kept these mementos for one very good reason. She'd never forgotten Adam Bartlett.

But she might have to forget him now.

As Adam drove north on Route 30 on Friday evening, he recalled again the e-mail he'd received from Mark when he'd awakened and Shawna had told him the news. He'd typed *Yes* with five exclamation points and written, *I knew we'd match. Will you come to see me before they start chemo?*

Adam had read the message inside the message. Mark was exuberant that he could have the transplant…but he was also scared. From the quiver in Danielle's voice when she'd phoned to tell him Mark had been admitted to the hospital around noon yesterday, Adam knew *she* was scared, too.

Adam tried to blank his mind to all of it as the countryside sped by. The drive to the farm outside of Warren took about thirty-five minutes. As Adam's tires crunched down the gravel lane, he thought about how well John had handled the farm and its upkeep. He kept up the paint on the barn as well as maintaining the house and the other buildings in good repair. Before he'd been hired on, Adam had had one of the out buildings renovated into a small utilitarian cabin, and that's where John lived. Now he'd be moving into the main house.

As Adam mounted the porch steps, he wasn't looking forward to this confrontation—he was sure that's what it would be. He and Sharon were like oil and water. Glancing to the side of the house, he saw her sedan was parked in front of the detached garage. His mom had wanted this to be a surprise, but if Sharon felt cornered, she'd resent him being there even more.

When Adam opened the wooden screen door, he looked toward the barn and caught a glimpse of John pitching hay into a stall.

It would no longer be the Bartlett farm. It would be the Pavlichek farm. He felt no stirring of regret at the difference.

After Adam knocked on the door, his mother opened it with a worried frown. Her short black hair was streaked with gray, but she wore makeup which was unusual for her. "Sharon saw you drive up."

"And?"

"She went up to her bedroom and shut the door." His mother fidgeted with the lapel of her housedress. "I really need you to talk to her, Adam. I've tried. John's tried. Even Rena tried by phone. But we just can't get through to her."

"If she keeps me locked out, there's not much I can do except talk through the door."

When his mother looked even more distressed, Adam added, "But I'll see what I can do."

The steps were steep, somewhat narrow, and Adam remembered all the times he'd run up and down them as a boy. The same floorboards still squeaked as he crossed the hall to Sharon's room and knocked.

"Sharon? It's Adam. Can we talk?"

When she opened the door, he realized he hadn't seen her since last summer. Since then she'd gotten her dyed blond hair cut shorter and gained some weight, maybe ten pounds. Still wearing her work clothes—navy slacks and a red and navy paisley blouse—she looked him over as if he were a door-to-door salesman. He'd left his suitcoat and tie in the car. He could tell she was assessing the clothes he wore and the probable cost. That was Sharon.

"Mom asked me to talk to you. Would you like to stay up here or go downstairs?"

"I don't want to talk anywhere. What could you have to say to me that would matter?"

Adam had always tried to maintain a politeness between them but too much was going on in his own life and he was tired of trying to be civil when she didn't put out any effort. "Your attitude belongs on a rebellious teenager, not on a grown woman. So why don't you act like an adult for a change and come down to the living room."

Surprised by his bluntness, it only took her a moment to find a quick comeback. "You think you're so smart. You've always thought you're so smart."

"Sharon, my being smart or not has nothing to do with this conversation. Why don't you want Mom to marry John?"

Apparently startled at his continued directness, she blurted out, "I don't want any man moving in here and taking Dad's place."

Before Adam had a chance to respond, she went on, "But you wouldn't know anything about how that feels because you hated Dad."

"I didn't—" He stopped short at the automatic protest. If he was going to get anywhere with Sharon, he had to be honest with her. "All right. Yes, I did hate him at times. He had a mean streak you didn't see. He showed it to me and he showed it to the livestock. You know as well as I do he only adopted me to have someone to work this farm for him. And after Delia died—"

Regretfully, Adam shook his head. "That's in the past now. If I hated him once, I don't anymore. He's gone and no matter what he was or wasn't, Mom deserves to be happy."

Sharon's expression lost some of its defiance. "I don't understand why Mom can't be happy the way things are. She and John—" Sharon stopped and her cheeks got red.

If his mother had been involved with John for a while, she obviously wanted to make it legal now. "Mom wants to be married and that's her right. Maybe if you can't accept it, if you can't accept John in this house, you should move off the farm and find your *own* life."

"That's easy for you to say," she muttered.

"Why?"

"Because you have more money than you know what to do with."

"I didn't have any money when I left for college."

"You had a scholarship."

"Yes, and it paid my tuition. I worked in pizza

joints for the rest. You do what you have to do to find your life, Sharon. You have a decent job. You can certainly afford an apartment. What's keeping you here?''

''*Mom's* keeping me here. After Dad died, she needed me here.''

''Maybe she did, but now maybe you both need something else. Think about it.''

Silence that had always seemed unbridgeable between them still seemed that way. Finally Sharon asked, ''Are you coming to the wedding?''

''I don't know. If Mom asks, I guess I'll try to be there.''

''She's not even going to have a real wedding. They're just going to a justice of the peace.''

''Anytime two people decide to spend the rest of their lives together and make promises to do that, I think it's a real wedding.''

''You know what, Adam? Just because you own your own company doesn't mean you know *everything.*''

Lord, did he know that! He almost smiled. ''I've never claimed to know everything, Sharon, but I do know if you don't support Mom in this marriage, it'll drive a wedge between the two of you.''

Suspecting Sharon wouldn't listen to anything else he had to say, he left her at her bedroom door and returned to the downstairs. She was one frustrating female he would never understand.

Adam's mother was putting a meat loaf in the oven when he entered the kitchen. After she closed the oven door, she asked, ''Can you stay for supper?''

Glancing at the ceramic teapot clock hanging on the wall, he shook his head. "I have to get back to town."

Peggy Bartlett sighed. "Did you make any progress with Sharon?"

"I don't know. I think she feels as if she's being disloyal to…Dad…if she accepts John into your life."

"That's ridiculous."

"That's how she feels."

His mother studied him for a moment. "Are you sure you have to get back?"

"I have to go to the hospital. There's a young boy I want to see there."

"You hate hospitals. You have ever since—"

They'd never talked about that day. "Yes, I do. But I'm going to have to change the way I've always thought about them."

She looked puzzled. "Why?"

"Because my biological father found me. His son needs a bone marrow transplant and I'm a perfect match."

It was obvious his mom was astonished by the news. "Your real father found you? My goodness, Adam."

"He has a family. I've got two half brothers and a half sister. Not only that, but—" he paused a moment "—did you know I had a twin?"

"A twin? No! We told you we didn't know anything much about your family. Just your mother's first name and that she was young and had died. That was all the information they'd give us."

"My father found my sister first. She lives on a

vineyard about two hours south of Portland. Apparently we're twins."

"Have you met her yet?"

"She was married recently and just returned from her honeymoon yesterday. I'm going to try to get hold of her."

"When did all this happen?"

"About a week and a half ago. Why?"

"A man called here, and he wanted to know if we had adopted a child from The Children's Connection Adoption Agency twenty-seven years ago. I told him we had. He went on to explain something about a fire and wanting to update records now. He asked where he could find you. I told him you had an unlisted phone number and I couldn't give that out, but when he pressed, I did say you were the boss of Novel Programs, Unlimited."

"So *that's* how he found me. He was a private investigator working for my father."

"If I had known he was a private investigator, I probably wouldn't have told him anything."

"Then I'm glad he didn't tell you. Mark's a great kid and I want to help him if I can."

"I hope everything turns out all right."

"So do I," Adam said in a low voice, and then he moved toward the doorway. "I'd better get going."

His mother followed him into the foyer. "Thanks for coming out here to talk to Sharon. I know she's not easy to deal with. I know...I know she and Rena weren't the best sisters."

When he was silent, she went on, "I know Owen and I weren't the best parents. Not to you, anyway. I felt I always had to do what Owen said, felt I had to stick by him. I didn't really want to care for another child, but he wanted a boy. We didn't adopt you for the right reasons and it showed. I'm glad your real father found you. Maybe you can find with him and his family what you never had with us. Maybe your twin can be the sister that Sharon and Rena never were."

Suddenly she clasped his arm. "I want you to know something, Adam. I'm proud of what you've done and who you've become. I'm not just saying that because of all the help you've given me. I think you've become a fine man."

His mother had never said anything like that to him before. He wondered if this new marriage she was going to enter into had changed her outlook on life...if she decided she deserved to live life instead of just letting it pass her by.

"Will you come to my wedding to John?" she asked.

"If you let me know where and when, I'll be there."

"Will you let me know when you go into the hospital? You will have to do that, won't you, to give bone marrow?"

"I'll let you know."

Then the woman who had always seemed a bit removed, who never seemed to know exactly what to say or do or how to act with him, gave him a hug.

Adam's heart felt lighter than it had felt in a long time as he drove to the hospital.

* * *

Since Mark's family was keeping him company, Adam didn't stay long. The eight-year-old had been subjected to tests all day, and Adam could easily see he was worn out. He'd simply wanted to stop in so Mark would know he was thinking about him.

After his visit, Danielle came outside the room with Adam, telling the others she was going to get something to drink. But as they walked partway down the hall, she turned to Adam. "They're going to start Mark's chemo on Monday. He doesn't know that yet."

"Do you know when they'll be ready for me?"

She shook her head. "It depends on how everything goes with Mark. Dr. Mason will contact you. Are you getting anxious about it?"

Anxious wasn't the word. He just wanted it all to be over and Mark to be okay. "Not really."

Danielle stuffed her hands into the pockets of her slacks. "We're going to go ahead with Shawna's party tomorrow night. We talked to Mark about it and he's okay with it. Chad's going to hook up one of those video phones so Mark can see what's going on."

"The party will help the weekend go faster," Adam offered.

Danielle nodded. "That's what we thought. Did Shawna tell you you're welcome to bring a guest?"

"She told me, but I'll probably come alone."

"We appreciate how you're keeping in touch with Mark, especially by e-mail. It's keeping his spirits up."

"Good. That's what I intended."

"Adam, Jared doesn't say much, but he appreciates everything you're doing, too."

Adam had learned a long time ago not to try to please a father figure. He really didn't care what Jared thought of him. Everything he did was aimed to help Mark. "I'm glad I got a chance to meet Chad tonight."

"So am I."

But as he left Danielle, Adam knew he'd had enough of family for the night and it was time to go back to the ranch and get his head together.

When Adam returned to the ranch, he took Thunder out on a short night ride. The temperature was in the fifties, and a warmer spell was predicted for next week.

After their ride, Adam walked Thunder to cool him down, then spent time grooming him, talking to him, going over the transplant procedure in his head.

It was ten o'clock when he got back to the house. Switching on the computer, he let his home page boot up while he checked the answering machine. At the same time, he flicked on the small television resting on the bookshelf to catch the local nightly news. He was getting deeply involved in research about cheetahs to design a new game for kids when he heard the sound of fire sirens coming from the TV.

Glancing up at the picture, he saw the local news anchor at the perimeter of a fire scene, motioning toward the firemen and a building.

Adam went instantly on alert and took a second,

more careful look at the building. That was Leigh's apartment house, wasn't it?

Turning up the volume, he heard the anchor say, "The fire at Turndale Apartment Complex began around 8:00 p.m. Mr. Benson in apartment 2C apparently removed bacon from a grease-filled pan and forgot to turn off the burner. Then he fell asleep in his recliner. Fortunately he awakened when a neighbor who smelled the smoke banged on his door. The fire had already enveloped his kitchen by then. Once the alarm was pulled, everyone evacuated the building. Only two apartments were seriously damaged, but several families are trying to find shelter for the night."

Adam shot up out of the chair and headed for his car. Were Leigh and her mother one of those families? Were they okay? Had they been taken to the hospital? Smoke inhalation could be serious.

Adam's foot was heavy on the accelerator as he drove into Portland and headed for Leigh's apartment complex. Of course he couldn't get anywhere near it. The street was blocked. After he parked, he jogged to the cordoned-off area. Smoke filled the air as firemen still hosed the roof.

Approaching one of the policemen who was holding a walkie-talkie in his hand, Adam asked, "Where are the families who got out? I want to make sure someone is safe."

The policeman eyed him. "You related?"

"A friend and her mother."

The officer nodded toward the parking lot. "Off in the far corner. We're still trying to figure out who's here and who isn't."

With a wave of thanks, Adam strode toward the parking lot searching every face as he went. When he saw a group of men and women, some with blankets over their shoulders milling about a large van, he ran toward it.

Leigh was standing beside a woman with an official-looking clipboard. He heard her say, "I don't know where we're going to go. We don't have any relatives here. Will we be able to take anything from the apartment?"

"I'm afraid not," the older woman with gray hair and a kind smile answered. "We'll give you a call when you can get back in."

Claire had been standing there, too, and now looked as upset as Leigh. "But we don't have anything. We don't have clothes for tomorrow or nightwear or even our toothbrushes. If we just wait until the firemen are finished—"

Adam stepped closer then. "Your apartment will be a mess from the smoke and the water damage. It might be hard to salvage anything."

Claire looked at him expectantly. "Adam! Maybe you can do something. I don't even have my purse." She turned away so he couldn't see how upset she really was.

Putting his hand on Leigh's shoulder, he could feel she was trembling and as upset as her mother. Looking toward the woman whose name tag said she was Esther Bradley, he asked, "Do they have to stay here?"

"No. They're accounted for. I just need a number where I can reach them."

"Do you have your cell phone?" he asked Leigh gently.

When she looked up at him, her eyes were shiny and she shook her head. "It was on the charger in the bedroom. Mom and I were in the living room watching TV when someone banged on the door."

Turning to Esther, he decided, "You can reach them at my number." He rattled it off.

Claire brushed one hand through her mussed hair. "What good is giving them your number going to do?"

Instead of answering, he asked, "Do you have any-place to go?"

Leigh and her mother exchanged a glance, then Leigh ventured, "A motel."

"Will your renter's insurance cover that?"

Again Leigh looked toward her mother.

Claire shook her head. "No, we don't know how long we're going to have to stay, either. I heard one of the firemen say our apartment was damaged the worst, next to Mr. Benson's. I guess we'll just have to put it all on Leigh's credit card. She managed to grab her purse on the way out."

"I have plenty of room at the ranch. Why don't you come and stay there until you find another place?"

It was almost a full minute before Claire replied, "We can't impose like that."

Leigh didn't say a word, and when Adam's gaze met hers, he wondered if he had just made the most foolish decision of his life. Even so, he couldn't go back now. "You won't be imposing. As I said, I have plenty of room. There are three bedrooms. You and

Leigh can have your own rooms. You'll even have a private bath. I'm at the office during the day and most evenings. It'll be better than a motel. You'll have a big-screen TV to watch.'' He tried to make a joke of it, hoping to bring a smile to their lips.

''We'd have to pay you,'' Claire insisted.

''No, you wouldn't. I won't take your money.'' When he saw she was about to protest again, he added, ''But I wouldn't mind a cooked meal, now and then, if that would make you feel better about staying there.''

''How far away is your ranch?'' Claire asked reluctantly.

''About twenty minutes out of town.''

''It would only be for a couple of days,'' Claire mused. She looked at Leigh. ''What do you think?''

''I think Adam's offer is kind and we don't have any choice, at least not for tonight. Maybe we can find another apartment quickly, but we need a place to crash in the meantime. Adam, are you sure about this?''

Whenever he looked at Leigh, he wasn't sure at all. But he was positive Claire would be a fine chaperone and she'd watch over her daughter. His primitive urges would just have to sit on the sidelines. ''Yes, I'm sure. Are you okay to drive?'' he asked Leigh.

''Yes, but I have to find my car. One of the policemen moved it.''

Claire said, ''I'll have to buy a few clothes someplace. So will you, Leigh.''

''I have an extra uniform in my locker, so I'll be okay with that. But we're going to need the necessities for tonight. Why don't we just take my car and stop on the way to Adam's. I know how to get there.''

''Are you sure you want to drive?'' Adam asked again.

Leigh nodded. ''I'm fine. And we'll need my car to get back and forth. Mom's car keys are still in her purse in the apartment.'' She clasped Adam's arm. ''Thank you.''

He knew they were in the middle of a fire scene. He knew people were milling about. He knew her mother was looking on. Yet none of that seemed to matter. Stroking his thumb along her cheek, he tried to deny everything he was feeling.

Knowing if he kept touching her, he'd want to touch her more, he dropped his hand. ''It's probably going to take you a while to get out of all this. I'll stop at the grocery store on my way home and stock up on food. Anything in particular you're hungry for?''

A smile tickled her lips. ''Chocolate marshmallow ice cream.''

''I should have guessed.'' It had always been her favorite, and when they had bought one cone and both licked from it…

Primitive urges belong on the sidelines, he reminded himself. ''Chocolate marshmallow ice cream, it is.''

As he stepped away from Leigh, he saw the way Claire was looking at them. It was a disapproving look, a worried look. Before she decided to go to a motel instead of Cedar Run, he made his way out of the bedlam, feeling strangely light, looking forward to having Leigh in his home.

Chapter Nine

Adam had just finished stowing away the food in his kitchen when his doorbell rang. Already having second thoughts about his invitation to the Peters women he hurried to the door and opened it wide. Both women looked tired beyond measure and carried the discount store shopping bags in their hands.

"Come on in."

Claire's gaze appraised his house as she came inside, and Adam supposed she was still having problems reconciling the teenager he'd been with the man he'd become.

"Let me hang up your coats," he offered, waiting for them to shed their outerwear.

But Leigh shook her head. "You don't want these

hanging with your good clothes. They smell like smoke. If we could just air them out somehow—''

''There's a clothes rack in the mudroom.''

''I need a good airing out as well as my coat,'' Claire told him with a small smile.

''Come on. I'll show you to your rooms. They have a connecting bath. If you want to get showers, you can.''

As they followed him, Adam made a quick decision on which rooms he'd put them in. There were three bedrooms. He showed Claire to hers first. After she went inside, she laid her bags on the quilted coverlet with its navy, burgundy and green mountain scene. The wrought-iron and rattan bed was a double. The rattan dresser and chest were roomy, and oak blinds at the windows were shut.

''This is nice, Adam. You have a beautiful home.''

''Thanks to a decorator,'' he admitted wryly. ''But I like it. It's comfortable, and that's what I'm looking for.'' He opened the door into the bathroom. ''The towels on the racks are fresh and there are more under the vanity.''

Claire nodded absently, and he sensed that she just wanted to be alone so she could absorb everything that had happened, get a hot shower and go to bed. ''Are you an early riser?'' she asked. ''I don't want to disturb you in the morning.''

''I'm usually up around six-thirty on weekends. I'll take care of Thunder and do some chores before I start coffee. You won't have to worry about disturbing me.''

Though his attention had been focused on Leigh's

mother, he was well aware Leigh was standing just outside the door, taking it all in. She looked pale and seemed much too quiet.

"After I show Leigh to her room, I'm going to turn in. Feel free to use the kitchen or watch TV." He guessed they'd be more comfortable if they had privacy.

Claire patted the bed. "I'm going to take a shower so I don't fall asleep in the tub. After that, I'll be asleep in about two minutes. I'll see you in the morning."

Adam had just reached the doorway when she added, "Thank you, Adam, for taking us in. We really appreciate it. I'll make breakfast in the morning if you'd like. Do you have eggs? Maybe some cheese?"

"Sure do. That sounds great. I hope you get a good night's sleep."

When Leigh followed him into her room, he heard the rustle of the bags she carried, the light sound of her footsteps on the hardwood floor. The guest bedroom he showed her to was beside his, but she didn't comment on that or the decor. This room was furnished in lodgepole pine furniture. The full-size bed was covered with a multicolored comforter of turquoise, red and yellow, but he wasn't sure she even noticed that as she went to the dresser and set her bags and purse on top of it. She rummaged in one of the white bags until she brought out a bottle of pink body gel and one of those net balls to use with it.

"Give me your coat," he suggested. "I'll take it to the mudroom."

Still without a word, she slipped it off and handed

it to him. Then he saw her shiver. She was wearing a burgundy sweatshirt and jeans. Wrapping her arms around herself, she looked as if she were cold.

Her back was still to him and he followed his instincts. Hanging her coat over the bed's footboard, he walked up behind her. "Leigh? What's wrong?"

In the shadows of the room he couldn't see her expression in the mirror.

"I know I shouldn't mind about things being gone. Mom and I are safe. Mr. Benson is safe. Everyone else in the complex is safe. But with the fire, smoke and water damage, we might have lost everything. There's no way to know until we can go back in."

His arms went around her then, but as he pulled her back against him, she shook her head. "I smell like smoke."

"I don't care." Tilting his chin down to her head, he just stood there holding her. Finally he tried to reassure her. "Maybe you'll be able to salvage something."

"That depends on what the fire took before they stopped it. I should have grabbed my jewelry box…some things from the closet."

"You had to get out, Leigh. That was more important."

"But the pearl necklace Mom gave me for graduation was important, and her photo albums, and the gifts the kids in the ward had given me, and… It's not that all of it is worth so much, but it all had memories attached."

Memories. Intangible visions. Feelings. Sensations

that came and went like wisps of smoke. He couldn't tell her she'd remember without the souvenirs.

Turning her to him, he took her face between his palms. "You'll make more memories and gather new souvenirs."

Her beautiful blue eyes were shiny with unshed tears. He realized she'd been strong all night for her mother. She was vulnerable now, and he could take advantage of that or do the right thing and walk away.

He just couldn't walk away so he chose the middle of the road. When he placed a gentle kiss on her lips, he felt her start and then her tremble.

Reluctantly, he pulled away. "I'm going to get you some brandy. It will warm you up and help relax you."

However, she shook her head. "I don't need brandy, Adam. A hot shower will work wonders."

"You're sure?"

"I'm positive."

Adam could hear the water running in the bathroom. "I'll let you get ready for bed."

After he picked up her coat, she asked, "Why did you come to the fire tonight?"

"I didn't put any thought into it. I saw the picture on television, realized your building was burning, and before I knew it I was in the car. I guess I wanted to make sure you were safe."

"I'm not used to having someone look out for me," she murmured. "Except for Mom."

"I think you look out for *her,* too."

Before he did take advantage of Leigh's vulnerability, before he did something they'd both regret, he went to the door. "If you need anything, I'll be in my room."

After he left Leigh standing in his guest bedroom, he knew with her in the room beside his, he wouldn't get any sleep tonight. He'd picture her in that bed. He'd think about all the things he'd like to be doing with her in a bed.

He was the one who needed the brandy.

Adam was hoisting a bag of feed and pouring it into a bin when Leigh came into the barn Saturday morning, took off her jacket and threw it over a stall. "It still smells smoky," she said, wrinkling her nose.

It was raining again, but she looked like sunshine in her jeans and yellow pullover sweater that she must have bought last night. Her hair was loose around her face, the way he liked it.

Thunder neighed at her and when she got closer, he did it again.

"Does that mean he's glad to see me?" she asked with a bright smile.

"Sure does."

"Can I pet him?"

"Go slowly. The same way as the first time."

Crossing to the horse's stall, she stood before the large stallion, just looking into his eyes, silently communicating with him. After she brought her hand up slowly, she laid it on top of the gate. In a few moments, Thunder lowered his head and snuffled her fingers. She laughed and gently stroked his nose.

"You seem in better spirits this morning," Adam

noted, finishing with the burlap sack and dropping it next to the feed bins.

"I'm trying to put it all in perspective. After Mom makes breakfast, we're going to go apartment hunting."

"I get the feeling she's uncomfortable staying here with me."

"Mom doesn't like to be beholden to anyone. She's hoping we can find something suitable today so we can get out of your hair."

Crossing to Leigh, he stood beside her and ran his hand down Thunder's neck. "Is that the way you feel? You want to get out of my hair?"

When she faced him, her gaze met his. "I always enjoyed being around you, Adam. That hasn't changed."

After Thunder whinnied, he pawed the ground, then turned to the other side of his stall.

"He seems restless," Leigh remarked.

"I'm going to take him out for a ride after breakfast."

"In the rain?"

Adam shrugged. "He likes it, and so do I. I have a slicker in the tack room. It'll keep me dry." Propping one booted foot on the first rung of the stall, he asked, "Are you going to Shawna's party tonight?"

"I thought I'd stop in. What about you?"

"I wouldn't miss it. I managed to get her tickets and a backstage pass to the 'NSYNC concert."

"She'll be thrilled."

After a moment he added, "And my sister Lissa

might be there tonight. I'd like to meet her. The only thing is—''

''What?''

''I hate to think of meeting her for the first time in the middle of a crowd.''

''Why don't you call her and make contact ahead of time? At least that way you might get a good feel for what she's like.''

''She was supposed to return from Scotland this week. I didn't know how soon I wanted to barge into her life.''

''If I had a brother out there who I'd never met, I'd want to hear from him as soon as I could.''

Unable to keep his hands to himself, he brushed a silky tendril of Leigh's hair behind her ear. ''Not all women are like you.''

''I hope not,'' she joked.

But he hadn't been joking when he'd said it. Leigh obviously cared deeply about everyone and everything in her world.

''Maybe I'll call her when I get back from my ride. Do you want to go together tonight?''

When she seemed a bit uncertain, he reassured her. ''I don't have any ulterior motives, Leigh. I like being with you, too. Since we're both going, we can do our part to conserve fuel.''

His suggestion brought another smile. ''All right. I'd like to go with you. Have you heard from Mark?''

''I visited him last night…before the fire. He's scared but he's facing this like an adult. Better than an adult. He just wants to get the whole thing over with. I'm going to stop in and see him again this afternoon. It might be the last time I can visit for a while. They'll move him into isolation tomorrow. Shawna told me that after the party, her mom's going to go to the hospital and stay overnight with Mark."

"That will be good for both of them."

With Leigh standing so close to him, he wanted to touch her again. The swish of Thunder's tail along with the pitter-patter of gentle rain on the roof were the only sounds in the barn. Leigh's sweater had a rounded neck, and her pulse point above it seemed to vibrate faster. His own heart was pounding harder.

"I can't be around you and not want to kiss you," he said hoarsely.

"I want you to kiss me." Her voice was no louder than the rustle of hay, but he heard it.

When he wrapped her into his arms, he didn't rush any of it. He wanted to savor inhaling her scent. He wanted to remember how fragile she felt held against him. When she looked up at him with eyes as blue as a beautiful clear sky, he wanted her in a way that was primal and aching and deep. He kissed her forehead and her cheeks and finally her mouth. She tasted of mint and coffee and every delicacy he could ever imagine. He was fully aroused as they took the moment and ran with it, melding to each other more completely. Rocking against her, he groaned from the pleasure. When her hands curled tightly on his shoulders, he knew he was giving her pleasure, too.

However, Thunder's snort alerted Adam that something had changed. An instant later, the barn door scraped open on its hinges. Adam prepared himself for the intrusion as he broke the kiss and pulled back but didn't take his arms from around Leigh.

"Are you two soon ready for breakfast? I made our first appointment for nine-thirty." Claire Peters's voice trailed off as she saw the two of them and guessed what they had been doing.

Leigh's color was high but she didn't skitter away, and Adam was glad about that. Instead she merely shifted in Adam's arms.

He answered Claire, "We're ready when you are."

"I suppose I interrupted something," Claire determined matter-of-factly.

Adam released Leigh now and answered for them both. "We were discussing the Cambrys' party tonight. We were both invited, and we're going together."

"I see." Claire didn't look happy about it, but she didn't say anything more, either. Adam guessed that Leigh was going to get an earful later.

For now, though, she smiled at her mother. "After we look at apartments, I need to shop for something simple to wear tonight."

"I'm sure we can find something," Claire decided, although she didn't sound as if her heart were in it.

Leigh touched Adam's arm, and with a smile said, "I'll help Mom with breakfast."

"I won't be long," he replied as he watched Leigh pick up her jacket and leave the barn with her mother.

Two hours later Adam had returned from his ride, still thinking about kissing Leigh. At breakfast their gazes had connected often. They were on the verge of something again, something that was going to hurt them both. He knew that and so did she, but they couldn't seem to help themselves.

As he groomed Thunder, he thought about the party at Jared's, about Leigh's suggestion to call Lissa. If she didn't want to answer the phone, she wouldn't pick up. If she didn't want to talk to him, he'd be able to hear it in her voice. Either way, he'd be prepared for tonight.

The legs of his jeans were wet from the ride but instead of going to the house to change first, he took his cell phone from his belt, searched for the number he'd entered after Jared had given it to him, and pressed Send.

"Hello?" It was a soft melodic voice that sounded a bit sleepy.

"Lissa Grayson?"

"Yes, I'm Lissa. Who's this?"

"Adam Bartlett."

There was a shocked silence, then an exuberant "Adam! Oh, my goodness. I'm so glad you called. I just got back yesterday and I'm not even out of bed yet. Well, I mean..."

He heard a male chuckle nearby.

Although he should feel awkward at this intrusion into her life, he suddenly felt relieved, and a smile came to his own lips. "I should have known better than to call before noon. You're a newlywed."

At that, she said, "Hold on a minute, Adam."

He heard a brief mumbled conversation and suspected she was telling her new husband who was calling. Then she returned to the phone. "Okay, I'm awake and I'm all yours. Are you going to Shawna's party tonight?"

"That's why I'm calling. A crowd didn't seem the best place to make introductions."

"I hadn't thought of that, but you're right. I can't wait to see what you look like. Ever since I heard I had a twin, my mind's been spinning."

"I know what you mean. Did you know that I'm a match for Mark?"

"Jared left the news on the machine here at the vineyard. I'm so glad. Everybody was so disappointed when I wasn't a match, and I felt as if I'd let them down somehow."

"Now you don't have to be worried about it. I know there's no guarantee the transplant will take, but if we all believe it will, that's got to help."

"I can't believe I'm actually talking to you! Jared called me in Scotland to tell me he'd met you. He said you're the CEO of a software company, but he didn't say much else. Are you single...married...involved?"

Lissa's excitement at finding him and wanting to know about his life created a joy inside of him as he'd never known. She had no ax to grind. She didn't want anything from him. She just wanted to get to know who he was.

Still...answering her question wasn't easy. "I'm single."

"Hmm," she said teasingly. "Do I hear something else attached to that?"

He laughed. "It's a long story."

"So, tell me about it. Sullivan went out with Barney. He's our dog."

It was odd, but Adam already felt as if he'd known Lissa for a lifetime. It was unlike him to confide his personal life to anyone, but she seemed to really care. "I have someone staying with me right now. I knew her in high school. She's a nurse at Portland General and has been the liaison during Mark's transplant process. There was a fire in her apartment building, and she and her mom had nowhere to go."

There were a few moments when Lissa seemed to be thinking about what he'd told her. "I think there's a lot you're leaving out since you haven't really told me if you're involved *now*."

"Leigh's coming with me to the party tonight. You can meet her and draw your own conclusions."

Lissa laughed. "I'll do that. I can't wait for you to meet Sullivan."

Then Lissa launched into the story of how she and Sullivan had met. Finally she revealed, "And the best news of all is, I'm going to have a baby. Just think, you haven't even known me a day and you're going to be an uncle!"

An uncle. A real sister. And Lissa cared. It all seemed surreal to Adam but he was slowly getting used to the idea. "Congratulations. You sound happy about it."

"We're both thrilled."

When Adam heard noises in the background again, the barking of an excited dog, he knew her new husband was back. "I won't tie you up any longer right now. Maybe we'll find some more time to talk tonight."

"You can bet we will. And I'm only two hours away, Adam. We can get together anytime we want."

He liked the sound of that. He liked the sound of Lissa, and he couldn't wait to meet her in person.

That evening, the Cambrys' house blazed with light. Cars were parked around the circular drive and on the macadam area beside the garage.

"Full house," Adam commented to Leigh as they walked up to the front door.

"Shawna told me they didn't only invite her friends, but some neighbors, too."

As always, Leigh looked pretty tonight. He could tell she'd shopped frugally and practically but she still looked elegant in her black slacks, white silk blouse and vest with multicolored fringe. On top of it all, she wore a red jacket. He'd seen the sale price on the sleeve before she'd removed it.

After his visit to Mark, he'd been running late, and they hadn't had much time to talk in the car. She had told him Claire had found two apartments she liked. The problem was, the one with the two bedrooms wouldn't be available for another month. The other had a nice location and a reasonable price, but only one bedroom. The one-bedroom apartment was available immediately.

A uniformed maid opened the door before Adam could even ring the bell. Chatter flowed out from inside, and as he and Leigh stepped into the living room, he saw Shawna surrounded by a crowd of her friends. She was wearing black leather slacks and a short pink top with little beads hanging all over it. When she spotted him, she waved.

As soon as the maid took Leigh's coat, Danielle came toward them, hands outstretched. ''I'm so glad you could come. The table in the dining room is loaded with food and there's dancing in the family room. Lissa isn't here yet,'' she said to Adam. ''She called, though. She and Sullivan are running a little late. Something about their dog splashed around in a mud puddle and they had to give him a bath.''

Adam was smiling as he guided Leigh toward the family room and the music.

''Did you call your sister?'' Leigh asked.

''Yes, I did. I can't wait to meet her.'' Adam had glanced into the dining room and now canvassed the family room. ''I don't see Jared. I wonder where he is.''

''Maybe he's running late for some reason, too.'' Leigh had brought a present for Shawna and now took it to a table heaped with gifts. *His* present for Shawna was tucked into his inside jacket pocket.

Adam was about to ask Leigh if she wanted to get something to eat when Shawna breezed in, her hand clasped in a boy's. He was tall and rangy looking. ''Adam and Leigh, I want you to meet Peter. Peter Bennett, my brother Adam and a friend of his, Leigh.''

The boy gave them an offhanded grin. ''Nice to meet you.''

''Nobody's dancing,'' Shawna said, looking around, seeing teenagers in one group of conversations and adults in another. She looked at Adam. ''If I put a slow one on, will you two dance?''

"Are you insinuating that I'm too old to enjoy a fast one?" he joked.

Her cheeks reddened. "No, but Peter prefers slow ones."

The boy was looking at Shawna as if he'd rather dance a slow dance with her someplace private. Adam wondered how Jared handled that. That was a part of being a father that would be damn tough.

He glanced over at Leigh. "A slow one okay with you?"

"That's fine with me."

Shawna went to the entertainment center and soon soft strains of a new pop idol's ballad poured from the speakers. It had been ten long years since Adam had danced with Leigh. Now he opened his arms to her.

When she placed her hand on his shoulder, he could feel its warmth through his suit coat. At least he thought he could. Her other hand was so small, so fragile in his, and he closed his hand around hers and brought it into his chest. When she looked up at him, everybody else in the room faded away. It was only the two of them and the music, her perfume and his cologne mingling, the heat of their bodies coming together. Other couples were dancing now, too, but Adam paid them no mind.

As his arm tightened around Leigh, his jaw brushed her temple. "Did your mother say anything about finding us in the barn this morning?"

Leigh's shoulders lifted and fell, then she looked up at him. Her face was only a few inches from his. "She's just worried about me."

"What's there to worry about?"

"She doesn't want me to get sidetracked."

"We're both responsible adults now, not teenagers. Even if we decided to get involved, we can take precautions."

"You mean against pregnancy," Leigh murmured.

"Yes."

The idea of an involvement and what it would mean wisped around them like a cloud. Pictures played in Adam's mind. Was he contemplating an affair with Leigh knowing he'd have to let her go in June?

Usually he could tell what Leigh was thinking, but now she turned her head away and rested it on his shoulder. Was she thinking about the heartache they'd be asking for? Was she imagining sleeping with him? Why was the timing always wrong for them?

One song stretched into two and Adam decided to stop thinking about the future and simply enjoy what was happening right now. Leigh was soft and fragrant and warm in his arms. He was aroused, and he suspected she was too from the flush on her cheeks, the sparkle in her eyes, the closeness of their bodies.

Then suddenly he felt a tap on his shoulder. When he turned, he saw Chad. The teenager had Jared's hair but resembled his mother. Beside him was a beautiful young woman, who looked a bit like Adam did himself.

Chad said somberly, "Adam, Lissa Grayson and her husband Sullivan. Sullivan and Lissa, meet Adam Bartlett and Leigh Peters."

Adam's heart raced as he released Leigh and turned to face Lissa. The next moment his twin was hugging him, and he knew he finally had a real family.

Chapter Ten

Twenty minutes later Adam decided he liked Sullivan as much as he liked Lissa. Her husband had a quick wit and an easy laugh. It was obvious he adored his new wife, and she loved him.

While Sullivan answered Leigh's interested questions about the vineyard, Lissa tugged Adam through sliding glass doors onto the patio, her long dark-brown hair flowing behind her. She pulled out one of the white wrought-iron chairs at a small round table, and he sat across from her. They just stared at each other for a while and then both of them laughed.

''You *do* look like me,'' Adam admitted with a smile.

''No, *you* look like *me*.'' Then her smile slipped away, and he saw that Lissa Grayson could be a very serious young woman, too. "Tell me how you grew up," she prompted.

"Why don't you go first." He'd never really talked about his background to anyone except Leigh, and it seemed odd to do it now. Lissa must have seen that he needed to get comfortable with the idea so she started slowly.

"The Cartwrights loved me. They always have and they always will. But my sister, their biological daughter, was so beautiful, so accomplished, so intelligent that I was always insecure. Until Sullivan came along. Then I felt beautiful and intelligent and special, too." She hesitated a few moments but then went on to tell Adam about growing up at the vineyard and the makeover Jared had helped her with. It seemed she'd connected with Jared, though she still thought of the Cartwrights as Mom and Dad.

She pushed her waist-length hair over her shoulder. Propping her elbow on the table, her chin in her palm, she said, "So now I want to know more about you. Are you and Leigh Peters involved?"

"Just because we were dancing doesn't mean we're involved."

"You were doing more than dancing. I saw the way you two were looking at each other. But if you don't want to talk about it, I'll understand."

Lissa was so ingenuous, so absolutely natural, and he saw that she wanted to know because some part of her already cared about him. Feeling more comfortable now, he told Lissa the story of how he and Leigh had met at her locker in high school, of the note she'd left him three months later. Somehow that led into his life with the Bartletts and how he'd always felt as if he were odd man out.

After he'd finished, she scolded, "You still didn't answer my question. *Are* you and Leigh involved now?" Lissa's green eyes were bright as she asked him for the truth.

"I'm telling myself I shouldn't get involved. I'm reminding myself she's leaving in June."

Just then Sullivan came through the sliding glass doors and onto the patio. Crossing to his wife, he laid his hand on her shoulder. "How are you feeling?"

"I think jetlag is setting in."

"Or pregnancy. Jared said we could stay the night if we'd like instead of driving back. That might be better for you."

"Maybe that *would* be a good idea. I'll give Mom and Dad a call. I'm sure they won't mind taking care of Barney tonight. He's going to love having a baby to romp with." She reached out and covered Adam's hand with hers. "You will be a *real* uncle, won't you? I want you to come visit often."

"I'll come. I'd like to have you and Sullivan out to the ranch. We'll set up a date after the transplant."

Leigh came to the door then, too. "I'm sorry to interrupt, but Jared would like all of you to come in. He wants to give a toast."

To his surprise Adam didn't feel as if Leigh were interrupting. He felt as if she belonged by his side. Yet he knew that wasn't going to happen. Still, as they went to the living room, he took her hand and she smiled up at him as if she were glad she was at the party with him.

As Adam and Leigh stood on the fringes of the crowd in the living room, a waiter made sure everyone had a drink. Jared draped his arm around Shawna's shoulders and ushered her toward the fireplace. There he handed her a glass. "Sparkling cider," he elaborated with a wink.

When she just rolled her eyes, everyone laughed.

Danielle and Chad came to stand beside him. They, too, had glasses in hand.

After Jared was sure he commanded all of his guests' attention, he raised his and addressed the crowd. "This is a happy occasion for us. Shawna has turned sixteen and she's definitely on her way to adulthood. We've never been more proud of her than we are right now. Shawna, happy sixteenth birthday."

After a round of applause, Jared still didn't move away from the fireplace. Rather, he waited until the applause died down, and then his gaze met Adam's.

"There's someone else here tonight who I'd like to introduce to you. I don't know if all of you have met him yet. He's giving us the greatest gift we could possibly imagine. Adam Bartlett is the man who will donate his bone marrow to Mark. He's a perfect match, and we want to toast him and his generosity in helping us save Mark's life."

Again everyone applauded and Adam soon found all eyes were on him. He raised his glass to Jared's, forced a smile and then took a swallow of his drink.

After the applause died down, everyone turned away and began mingling again. A few of the guests introduced themselves to Adam, most were friends or neighbors of Jared's family. They kept telling him what a wonderful thing he was doing, and Adam felt awkward about all of it.

Standing beside Adam, Leigh watched him go still and turn inward. Whether he wanted to admit it or not, she was sure he was hoping Jared Cambry would be the father he never had. But Jared had just blown that idea to bits. He hadn't acknowledged Adam as his son, and she could see the effects of that in Adam's rigid stance as well as in his forced smile as he spoke to Jared's friends and neighbors. Leigh ached for him and understood the child inside of him who'd wanted Owen Bartlett to accept him as a real son. She didn't know what she would have done as she was growing up if she hadn't had her mother's support. Unlike her, Adam had gone it alone from an early age. She admired him for that, but she'd also seen the toll it had taken on him.

After the well-wishers had moved away, he leaned toward Leigh. "I want to find Shawna again and give her her birthday present. Then I'll be ready to leave. Will you?"

"Whenever you're ready." She'd attached a card to her birthday present for Shawna that was on the table in the family room. It wasn't necessary for her to be here when Shawna opened it. The trendy purse had caught Leigh's eye and she hoped Shawna liked it. On the other hand, she couldn't wait to see Shawna's face when Adam gave her his gift.

It took a few moments for them to find and snag Shawna.

"Do you want to do this alone?" Leigh asked

Adam in a low voice as he guided Shawna toward a quiet corner.

"No. I want you to enjoy her reaction, too."

Shawna stopped beside an indoor palm. She was flushed and happy and excited, enjoying every minute of her party. Enthusiasm bubbled over as she asked, "You're not leaving are you?"

"Soon. I wanted to give you your present first. I was afraid it would get lost if I put it on the table."

"You didn't have to bring a present. Just having you here was a gift."

Leigh could see that Shawna's words went a long way to making up for what her father hadn't said to Adam.

"A sixteenth birthday deserves something memorable." Adam took an envelope from his inside jacket pocket. "I thought you might enjoy these."

As Shawna took the envelope from him, she looked puzzled. It was a legal-size white envelope giving no hint as to what it held. When she pulled out the four tickets inside and a square piece of paper, she looked up at them in astonishment. "The 'NSYNC concert! Oh, my gosh! They were sold out before I could get home from school and call. How did you get these?"

"I just happen to know their road manager. My partner invited him to one of his parties."

"Oh, my gosh," she said again. "And is this a backstage pass?"

"It sure is. You'll have a chance to talk with them for a few minutes. Make sure you have your camera so a friend can snap a picture."

"I can take three friends." Suddenly she threw her

arms around Adam's neck and gave him a big hug. "This is *so* cool. Wait till I tell Mark." After she released Adam, she stepped away. "Dad's going to use the video phone and call Mark. Are you sticking around for that?"

"No. Leigh and I are going to leave now. You can tell Mark I'll e-mail him later."

"I'm glad Mom's going to the hospital and staying with him tonight, then he won't feel alone." After she looked down at the tickets again, she glanced back at Adam. "How did it go with you and Lissa?"

"I like her. A lot. We're going to get together after the transplant."

A few minutes later, when Shawna decided she wanted to show her mom the tickets, Adam and Leigh went with her to say goodbye. They found Lissa, too, and Leigh could see that Adam and his twin were on their way to developing a lasting bond.

On the drive back to the ranch, Adam was quiet and Leigh left him to his thoughts. He had a lot on his mind—Mark's bone marrow transplant, his own procedure, the new family he'd met.

When they reached Cedar Run, Adam pulled into the garage. After they went in the side door to the kitchen, they found all the lights still on and the TV playing. But when Leigh's mother heard them, she switched it off.

"Mom. I'm surprised you're still up."

"It's only eleven. I had a call earlier and I needed to discuss it with you."

Shrugging out of his suit jacket, Adam said, "I'll say good-night."

But Claire stopped him. "No, Adam. Stay. This concerns you, too. The apartment manager called—the one who had that apartment we liked with one bedroom. If we don't want it, she has someone who does. I like the section of town it was in, and it was so bright and cheerful. We'll be cramped until you go to school but then you'll be in Cleveland, and I'll be alone. I'd like to take it. Adam will have his place back, and we can get settled in."

Adam looked at Leigh. "Do you have a place in Cleveland yet?"

"Yes. I flew out over the President's Holiday. I'll be sharing an apartment with two other women. Their roommate is moving out at the end of May, and I'll be taking her place."

"I had another call, too," Claire said. "We can get into our old apartment tomorrow and salvage what we can. If we take this apartment, we'll have someplace to move in to."

"It sounds as if your mind's made up." Leigh didn't know how she felt about feeling like a guest at her mother's. But that's what she'd be.

"I guess my mind *is* made up. It will be hard for you now, not having a room of your own. But the one-bedroom is spacious, and we can probably fit your twin bed in with my double. That way you'll have a place to sleep when you come home over holidays, too."

Besides all the good reasons she'd listed, Leigh knew her mother didn't like imposing on Adam. She also knew her mom had a budget she had to adhere to. Yet Leigh felt misplaced, as if she wouldn't really have a home until she got to Cleveland. Then she thought about everything else that would be happening this week—Mark's chemo, Adam being admitted to the hospital…

Suddenly Adam made a suggestion that took Leigh by surprise. "If you're going to be crowded, Leigh, you can stay here until you leave for Cleveland. I've got plenty of room."

Stunned silence met his suggestion until Claire recovered. "That's not a good idea," she snapped.

But Leigh wasn't as quick to dismiss it for a multitude of reasons. "Adam's offer might solve all our problems, Mom. Mark's transplant will most likely happen this coming week. I want to be here with Adam. He'll need someone to drive him home after his bone marrow extraction. And someone should really be here with him at least for the day he's released."

"That's a lot different from staying until June. What would people say?" Claire insisted, obviously concerned with more than propriety.

"What people, Mom? What I do is no one's business but mine."

At this point Adam intervened. "Leigh wouldn't be living with me, per se, Ms. Peters. She'd be sharing my house. We probably won't even see that much of each other with our work schedules. I didn't bring it up to cause friction. I just thought if it was a solution, maybe we should consider it. As far as the bone marrow donation goes, Dylan can drive me home. I'm sure I'll be fine. If you want to stay because it's practical for you to do that, Leigh, the invitation is open. Don't base your decision on what's happening with me. Okay?''

Adam's intent was clear. He was telling her he didn't need her. He was just offering her an alternative to living in a one-bedroom apartment with her mother...an alternative she was seriously considering.

''I'm sure you want to discuss this between the two of you,'' Adam added. ''I'll be in my office. I'm going to e-mail Mark and then work on a few scheduling details for next week.''

As Adam hooked his suit coat over his shoulder and strode through the living room to his den, he looked casual and relaxed as if Leigh's decision didn't matter to him at all. Did he care if she stayed with him or didn't he?

Slipping off her jacket, she went to the foyer closet and hung it up.

When she returned to the living room, her mother was waiting expectantly. ''You're not seriously considering staying here with *him,* are you?''

If her mother was trying to make Adam faceless for her, she wouldn't be able to do it. ''As I said, he might need me.''

''You can't expect me to believe that if you stay here, you're simply going to be housemates.''

She honestly didn't know what would happen between her and Adam. But she did know one thing. ''I'm not going to give up my dreams simply because I decide to stay with him.''

''I'm glad to hear it. But the temptation's going to be there, and you *will* get hurt.''

Was she ready to face the fact she might? She was.

Her expression must have told her mother what she was thinking. Shooting to her feet, Claire shook her head vigorously. "You can't tell me you're entertaining the idea of an affair. Leigh, didn't I teach you better than that?"

"You can't live my life for me, Mom. I know what you taught me. I know what I believe. But I also know my heart is telling me to stay here with Adam. Part of me has always wondered about him...wondered if he could open up...wondered if he could ever share what he was feeling."

"What if he can do those things? What if you come under his spell again?"

A smile came to her lips. "Oh, Mom. Adam is no sorcerer. I control my own destiny. Can't you see I need the chance to make my own decisions and make my own mistakes?"

"I don't want you to have to *make* mistakes. I made one that cost me my future. *Your* future could be brilliant. Please don't throw that away to live in the moment."

"I'm not going to throw anything away. I'll help you sort through your things and move into your new place. I'll visit you often whenever you'd like. But I'm going to move in here until I leave, and I'm going to tell Adam right now."

Her mother was used to getting the last word, but Leigh didn't stay around to hear it this time. She didn't stay around to be convinced that not seeing Adam anymore would be the better thing to do. Logic just didn't fit into this equation anymore. She had to go with her instincts, and her instincts were telling her to stay.

Her knock on Adam's door was decisive. She heard him call, "Come in." Opening it, she saw him sitting at the computer, his e-mail program on the screen. "Did you hear from Mark?"

"Sure did. And he said his dad's video-phone worked. Shawna showed him her tickets and he's jealous, but she's going to take pictures and maybe get an autograph for him with her backstage pass."

Adam motioned to the end of the letter. "Danielle just got there, and they're getting ready to turn in. I'm glad she's going to be there tonight. It'll do them both a lot of good."

Swiveling away from the computer then, Adam faced her. "I didn't hear any yelling and screaming coming from the living room. Are you and your mom okay? Maybe I should have waited and asked you privately, but I wanted to be straightforward about the offer."

There was no point going into how her mother felt. "I accept your invitation to stay, Adam."

Rising to his feet, he approached her. "I meant what I said about being housemates, not living together. There are no strings attached to this, Leigh."

He was close and he was sexy and she could so vividly remember dancing with him.

"And if you're here after I donate bone marrow, I *don't* need a nursemaid."

Adam had always had a tremendous amount of pride and she respected that. "But you won't mind if I make supper, will you? Just as a thank-you for letting me stay. I *am* going to pay you rent."

"No, you're not."

This time *her* pride was at stake. ''There's no discussion on this, Adam.''

''Sure there is. I don't want your money. Throw it into a savings account for things you'll need. Or help your mom buy new furniture.''

''I can't stay here for free.''

''Why not?''

His eyes were filled with humor and something more serious. His tie was undone, hanging around his shirt collar. He'd rolled up his sleeves and unbuttoned the top two buttons of his shirt. He was so unbearably male.

''Because...'' She forgot what she was going to say when Adam came even closer...when he bent his head and kissed her. It was a fleeting kiss as their kisses went, yet it was thoroughly arousing nevertheless. When he backed away, she knew he knew it.

Finding her voice, she managed, ''I have to feel I'm contributing. What if I make sure there's always something edible in the refrigerator, whether it's from the deli or something I cook?''

After considering her suggestion, he smiled, ''That would be a change. I'm a connoisseur of peanut butter and stale crackers.''

''Good. That takes care of that.'' She glanced at the file folder open on his desk. ''Will you be up for a while?''

''I have e-mail to take care of.''

''Then I'll see you in the morning.''

''In the morning,'' Adam agreed.

When Leigh left his office, she thought about being

in the house with him alone. What if her mother hadn't been here tonight? Would he still have ended the kiss?

After tomorrow she'd know.

On Friday morning Leigh took her break early to check on Adam. He'd gotten a call on Wednesday that his harvesting and Mark's transplant were set for today. They had driven in early this morning from the ranch so Adam could register around seven-thirty. Her shift started at eight. After they'd separated in the lobby and she'd wished him good luck, he'd given her a thumbs-up sign.

When she'd accepted his invitation to stay at his house, she thought they might talk more and become closer. But since Saturday night, Adam had been keeping his distance. With his pickup truck, he'd helped her and her mother move everything salvageable into her mom's new apartment on Sunday. Yet after Sunday, they'd pretty much gone their separate ways. Adam had worked late every night, and she wondered if he was doing it to distract himself from Mark and the transplant or to stay away from her.

Before Leigh had taken a break, she'd called Patient Registration for the number of Adam's private room. Hurrying down the hall, she found the number, then hesitated an instant outside the door. Finally she knocked before pushing it open. She'd expected to see him dressed in a hospital gown and lying on the bed. Instead, he was still wearing a polo shirt and jeans and pacing the room.

"Adam. I thought they'd be prepping you."

"I thought so, too," he muttered with a dark expression. ''But there's been a delay. Did you see Mark this morning?''

''I can't go in to see him, but I checked on his condition.''

''And?'' Adam's eyes said he wanted her to tell the truth.

''And he needs your bone marrow desperately. His abnormal cells have been destroyed, but normal cells have been destroyed, too. Have you heard from Danielle or Shawna?''

''Danielle e-mailed me last night. She's not saying it, but she's scared to death this won't help, that the transplant won't take. She's afraid he might get an infection even with all the precautions. And damn it, Leigh, I can't tell her not to worry because I'm worried, too.''

She could see he was, but she suspected there was more to it than that. Visiting Mark had been one thing, getting through today with the doctors poking, prodding and handling him was another.

Eyeing the hospital gown on the corner of the bed, she gently chided, ''You should get changed. They'll want to set up your IV soon—''

''I'm not getting into that damned hospital gown until it's necessary.''

Keeping her voice calm, she asked, ''Have you spoken with the anesthesiologist yet?''

''Yes, he was here about five minutes ago.'' With a disgusted look, Adam eyed the hospital gown again, then blew out a breath. ''All right. I'll get ready. But I'm not getting into bed until they want to knock me out.''

"I can try to find somebody to cover for me if you want me to stay."

"No!" was his immediate reply. "I don't need you here, Leigh. I don't need someone to hold my hand. I just want to get all of it over with."

If he didn't need her here, he didn't need her in his life. Was he just being kind by asking her to stay at the ranch with him? Maybe he was just trying to mend fences that had been too broken to repair. That had been his message this week. If she were smart, she'd listen to it.

But she cared too much about him to act indifferent. "I'll stop in before I leave tonight to see how the procedure went. You should be awake by then."

"You don't have to stop in. I'll call you in the morning and tell you what time I'm being discharged. Are you sure you don't mind driving in for me tomorrow? Dylan could take me home."

"I'm off for the weekend, and I really have nothing to do. Mom's apartment is pretty much together now so I'll be around all day if you need me."

Before he could say again that he didn't, in spite of his gruff attitude, she took a step toward him, stood on tiptoe and kissed him on the cheek. "That's for good luck. I'm sure everything will go smoothly. Just remember I'll be thinking about you as well as Mark, and I'm sure the Cambry family will be, too."

Looking down at her, he suddenly enfolded her into his arms and brought her close for a moment. As he held her, she could feel the beat of his heart.

Abruptly he released her and stepped away. When she gazed into his eyes, she saw the turmoil there and knew he was remembering another day and another time, Delia, and everything that had happened with the medical personnel.

"Good people work here, Adam. Trust them."

Then she left his room...because tears were too close to the surface, because she cared too much, because she was falling in love with Adam Bartlett all over again.

Chapter Eleven

When Leigh arrived at the hospital Saturday morning to pick up Adam, he looked ready to erupt.

"They're telling me the nurse has to wheel me down in the wheelchair like some invalid! Can you believe it?"

In spite of herself, Leigh felt a smile trying to burst from inside her. Adam's procedure had been textbook perfect. Marrow had been extracted from the back of his hip bones. It had taken the doctor an hour and a half to harvest as much as he needed.

She'd called the head nurse on duty last night and found out that Adam had grumbled and barked when the nurse had to remove his bandage and check the area. The doctor's orders stated he should stay in bed last night, and he'd agreed with the nurses about that.

Still, the head nurse had checked on him often to make sure he was listening. They'd supplied him with ice packs every hour, and Leigh knew he was supposed to use them for forty-eight hours, then heat if he still had pain and swelling. Antibiotics and pain medication had been ordered along with a sleeping pill. Thank goodness Adam had taken the antibiotic, although he'd refused the rest. Another of Leigh's friends on his floor had reported that he was listening to orders to drink a lot of liquids, so Leigh had stopped at the grocery store, buying three different kinds of juices as well as wholesome food. As with any procedure, infection could set in and she intended to watch him carefully for a fever, swelling or any trouble breathing.

"Well, I can see you came through the harvesting just fine, but your mood hasn't improved," she noted dryly.

Although she'd never quite seen Adam scowl before, she realized he was doing it now. Dressed in a football jersey and jeans, he moved a bit gingerly as he went to sit in the wheelchair. "Let's just get out of here. Any news on Mark? I feel isolated without my computer."

For Mark, the transplant had probably been the easiest part of his ordeal. The marrow had been introduced into his body through an IV. "He's doing as well as can be expected."

"I'm getting so tired of hearing hospital-speak," Adam grumbled.

"Adam, you know that's all they can tell us. It's going to be two to four weeks before we have real news on whether the transplant took. You're going to have to be patient just like the Cambrys."

"I'm thin on patience right now."

Maintaining her calm, she offered, "Then I guess we'll have to work on that today, won't we?"

She thought he might give her the I-don't-need-a-nurse speech, but instead he remained silent as if he knew that was his best course. Obviously, Adam was one of those men who did *not* make a good patient.

With a sunny smile, a nurse breezed into the room, clutching an instruction sheet in her hand. "You'll be staying with him?" she asked Leigh now.

"Yes. Unless he orders me off his property," she added with a smile, hoping to coax one from him.

His nurse's voice was enthusiastic and clear. "Here are his instructions, not anything complicated. You know what to look for. Make sure he takes the antibiotics and drinks plenty of liquids. He should use ice fifteen to twenty minutes every hour as needed. Switch over to heat tomorrow."

"I'm right here," Adam interrupted, obvious tension edging his tone. "You already told me all this. I even signed a paper that I understood it."

The nurse ignored him and handed Leigh a bag that had been sent up from the hospital pharmacy. "There's an antibiotic and pain medication in there."

After Leigh took the bag, the nurse went around to the back of the wheelchair. "All right, the gentleman wants to leave. Let's make it happen."

When Adam just rolled his eyes, Leigh suppressed another smile.

* * *

After Leigh parked in Adam's driveway, he got out of her Neon almost as quickly as she did. While she watched, he strode to the door with the movement of a man who was acting as if he was perfectly fine. He wasn't. She'd seen him surreptitiously shifting in his seat during the ride. Since the bone marrow extraction, she knew he'd felt as if he'd taken a bad fall.

To her dismay, after Adam unlocked the door, he started for his office. "I'm going to call my mother to tell her everything went okay, then work for a while." The look he gave her dared her to argue with him.

Knowing that argument would be useless, she offered, "I picked up three ice packs at the drugstore last night. They're in the freezer. I also bought a heat pack for the microwave."

She thought he might claim he didn't need those, either. Instead, he went to the kitchen and took two bills from his wallet, placing them on the table. "That should cover it." Then he took an ice pack from the freezer and went to his office.

Leaving Adam to his own devices for the time being, Leigh prepared lunch. Good food would help his recovery. After she put salmon in the oven to broil, she steamed asparagus and sliced a cantaloupe. Everything was ready when the microwave beeped, signaling the rice was finished.

When Leigh went to Adam's den to call him, he was still using the ice pack and staring at the computer screen. She suspected the pain was spoiling his concentration, but he wouldn't admit it.

To her chagrin, all of her attempts at conversation

were thwarted during lunch. She'd had enough psych classes to know that more was going on here than Adam's reaction to a medical procedure.

As he pushed his plate away and stood, she quickly cleared the table. "I think we should talk."

He eyed her warily. "About what?"

"About what's bothering you. It's obvious something is. Are you sorry you asked me to stay with you? Because if you are, I can still move in with Mom."

Running his hand through his hair, he leaned back against the counter and winced. "Damn," he muttered.

"That's exactly what I mean, Adam. You should be resting. You'll recover quicker if you do. Would you be resting if I weren't here?"

With a sigh, he admitted, "Probably. Maybe. I don't know. I just know I don't like anybody seeing me in a hospital gown or lying in a bed, especially you."

"Why, especially me? I'm a nurse, for goodness sakes."

"You're a *woman.* A woman who—" He shook his head. "I don't want you to see me as anything but strong."

"This is an ego thing?" she asked in amazement.

He flushed slightly. "If you want to call it that. I'm never sick. I don't take drugs. I've done everything in my power to stay out of hospitals. For the past three weeks, I've been inside Portland General enough to last me a lifetime."

So *that* was the problem. There was even more to it than that, she guessed. "Adam, I know what you went through. I know they took your vitals and hooked you up to a monitor and IV. I know you felt powerless as they gave you anesthesia, and you hated the nurses checking on you afterward. I know it brought everything back about that day in the hospital with Delia. Don't you realize if you talk about it, it will help? Keeping it all bottled up inside just makes everything worse."

After he rubbed his hand across his forehead, his gaze met hers again. "The whole experience brought back every bad memory I'd locked away. I recalled everything I saw that day...everything I felt. And after I woke up in recovery, all I could think about was Mark. What if my bone marrow doesn't take? What if it's not good enough?"

"Oh, Adam." She went to him then, put her arms around him and hugged him.

After a moment his arms went around her, too. "I didn't mean to be such a bear," he murmured. "I just wanted everyone to go away. I wanted to crawl into a cave and pull a boulder in front of the opening. I knew it would all pass eventually, but it's not passing quickly enough."

Leaning away, she looked up at him. "It won't pass if you don't talk about it. It will just gnaw at you and stay alive and resurface in the future. Isn't that what it's done since you were a kid?"

"I suppose so. But it's not easy to talk about, so I can't do it with just anyone."

"So talk about it with me."

He closed his eyes then and she suspected that if and when he talked about it with her, he felt vulnerable. He felt as if he were letting his guard down, and he didn't seem to want to do that.

"Even if I don't talk about it," he insisted, "I'm glad you're here. Believe it or not, having you at Cedar Run does make it all easier."

Relief flooded through her. "Good. Then I'm glad I'm here. Now would you consider taking one of those pain pills and resting?"

"You're sure that's going to help me recover faster?" he asked with some humor in his eyes now.

"I'm positive. You're in excellent condition and—"

"You've noticed that?" he asked with a smile.

She couldn't help the heat that came into her cheeks. "I've noticed."

When he took her face between his hands, he admitted, "I've been trying to stay away from you. I told you there were no strings attached to your staying here, and I don't want you to think I've changed my mind about that. But every time I'm near you, I want to kiss you."

She wanted to kiss him. He must have seen that because his lips settled on hers with demand and purpose and the intent to find some satisfaction or at least a distraction. After a long while, he broke away.

Forcing a smile, he decided, "I'm going to listen to my nurse's advice." Going over to the counter, he took out one of the vials and popped the lid.

Though Adam's words had pleased her, Leigh wondered if he could ever really let his guard down with her...if he'd ever really trust her again.

* * *

Leigh's company soothed Adam in a way nothing ever had, and he remembered again how much he'd enjoyed being with her when they were kids. He did sleep most of Saturday. On Sunday, when Leigh made a big breakfast, he found he was actually hungry. Checking his computer wasn't such a chore and he found an e-mail from Danielle, assuring him that Mark was holding his own. That was all they could expect right now. The news should have satisfied Adam, but it didn't.

To keep his mind off of Mark, Leigh played chess with Adam and watched an old movie on TV. After checking to make sure he didn't mind, she went to visit with her mother for a while.

When she left, the house felt empty. Adam found he liked having her coat hanging in the closet next to his. He liked seeing her face at breakfast. He liked hearing her sweet voice call to him from another room. Yet he knew he couldn't like any of it too much. Although kissing her was never far from his mind, he didn't act on any impulses.

By Monday Adam was feeling better but decided to work at home. He found himself looking forward to Leigh returning to the ranch after she finished at the hospital…to having supper with her. He was studying sales figures in foreign markets when she came home. Her step was light as she walked down the hall and peeked into his office.

"Busy?" she asked.

He turned away from the screen. "I can take a break. Any word on Mark?"

"Nothing's changed. I spoke with Danielle for a while, though. She's being so strong for all of them. Jared can't bear to hang around the hospital, but she feels that she can't leave. I convinced her to at least take a walk in the sunshine. When she came back, she had gotten a candy bar from a machine."

"Jared should make sure she's eating. He should be there for her."

"Everyone handles these kinds of situations differently. He's coming in tonight to spend the evening with her."

Was he judging Jared Cambry unfairly? What would he himself do in that situation?

He didn't know.

"Did you get the mail?" Leigh asked him.

"I didn't even think about it. I have to go out to feed Thunder in a little while. I can get it then." His gardener had taken care of Thunder over the weekend.

"How are you feeling?"

"Better. I didn't take pain meds today. I needed to see these figures clearly on the computer."

"They didn't affect your cognitive skills at all. You beat me at chess."

"I think that's just because I've played more often than you have. I'll be finished here shortly. I feel a lot better if I don't stay in one position too long. After Rodney took care of Thunder this morning, I told him I could handle him now."

"I think I'll walk down to the mailbox and get the mail. It's such a beautiful day and it'll help me clear my head."

"Of hospital smells?" he joked.

She gave him a weak smile. "No. We have a little girl on the ward who's not doing so well. I just need to get some distance."

"I admire the work you do," Adam said sincerely.

"I usually love it. Today was just...hard."

He might have gone to her then. He might have taken her into his arms and kissed the vestiges of the day away. But she turned quickly and headed for the living room, and he remembered what she'd said about needing distance. He felt each day they were becoming more connected. If he comforted her now, it would just be another string binding them together. They were eventually going to have to cut all those strings, and it wasn't going to feel good to do it.

Leigh took in huge lungfuls of air as she walked down the lane toward the mailbox, the end-of-the-day sun shining on her head. Tears had been too close to the surface in Adam's den and she hadn't wanted him to feel obligated to listen or to comfort.

As she walked, the wind tossed her hair, and she tried to put everything in perspective. By the time she reached the mailbox, she felt as if she'd gotten her equilibrium back, at least where Adam was concerned.

Pulling open the mailbox, she found three bills for him and a long, legal-looking envelope for her that had been forwarded. Tucking Adam's bills into the pocket of her jacket she quickly opened her envelope. Removing the letter, she unfolded it and read it quickly. She'd received a full scholarship to Case Western!

A full scholarship. That meant she wouldn't be as

tied down with loans after she graduated, though she still had those from undergrad school to pay.

She walked much more slowly up the lane than she had walked to the mailbox. Her future was unfolding. So why didn't she feel heady with excitement? Bubbling over with enthusiasm? Impatient to call her mother and tell her?

Instead of going to the house, she stopped by the corral to watch Thunder. Listening to her heart, she knew the reason the scholarship didn't bring her the joy it should have.

Adam.

While she stood at the fence, she watched Thunder run through the grass. A gust of wind caught her hood and whipped it to one side. As she made sure Adam's bills were secure in her pocket, she dropped her letter. The next gust spun it, dancing it into the corral. Believing she'd need that letter for verification of the scholarship, she hurriedly crawled through the fence into the corral.

As if it were playing a game with her, the breeze swirled the letter two feet away and then a few feet more. Finally Leigh snatched it, then raised her head to find Adam jogging toward her and calling to her.

''Get out of there, Leigh. Out of there!'' His words were loud and harsh.

She wanted to tell him he shouldn't be running. He was pointing, too, and she realized he was motioning to Thunder.

Then she got it.

The corral...an unpredictable stallion...what had happened to Delia.

Glancing over her shoulder, she saw Thunder was racing toward her. Deep in her soul, she didn't think the big horse would hurt her. She'd made friends with him, gone to the barn to talk to him often. Still, she hurried the ten feet to the fence and slipped between the rungs, breathless.

"I told you never to go into the corral with Thunder unless I was with you," Adam said furiously.

The beautiful black horse came up to them at the fence, snorted, and took off again the way he had come.

"I know you did, but the wind blew my letter inside."

"I don't care what it blew inside, Leigh. The next time, you let it go. The next time, you come get me. You know what happened to Delia." Then as if he couldn't stand to remember, as if he couldn't stand to look at her and be reminded of what had happened when he was a boy, he turned and strode toward the house.

Running after him, she clasped his arm. "Adam, I'm sorry."

"Sorry wouldn't have been enough if I had to call an ambulance and a team of doctors had to put you back together again." Pulling away from her touch, he went inside and she followed.

He was in the kitchen putting on a pot of coffee to brew when she came in, took his bills from her jacket and hung the coat in the closet. Joining him in the kitchen, she laid the envelopes on the table.

Their gazes met and all the anger seemed to ebb out of Adam, replaced instead by an intense concern. Raking his hand through his thick, brown hair, he said hoarsely, ''I don't want you to get hurt.''

She moved closer to him and murmured, ''I know you don't.'' She longed to touch him with the freedom of a lover, with the freedom of a woman who belonged to him, but neither applied to her. Instead she asked, ''Are you hurting after that run?''

''Is that the nurse asking?''

''No, it's your friend asking.'' She knew they were that now, if nothing else.

Tipping her chin up with his thumb, he responded, ''We've always been beyond friends, Leigh, and I've never known why.''

''Some people just…connect when they meet.''

''We didn't just connect, we sizzled. We still do. We sizzle when we're standing this close. We sizzle whenever I touch you.''

He brushed the back of his hand down her cheek and she felt her whole body tremble.

''We sizzle when you look at me with those big, blue eyes and I just want to get lost in them.''

''Oh, Adam…''

''We sizzle when my lips get anywhere near yours.''

As his words became actions, the sizzle between them was a mixture of chemistry, emotion, and past history. As Adam kissed her this time, his hands passed over her breasts. Through her silky blouse and her filmy bra, his touch was fire. Her nipples hardened and her breath caught.

As if he knew exactly what was happening to her, his tongue seduced her mouth while his thumb teased her nipple. The pleasure was so excruciatingly sweet, her knees felt weak. Backed up against the counter, she was grateful for the support.

"Do you know how much you distract me?" he broke the kiss to murmur in her ear. "Do you know how much you make me forget about everything else going on?"

"Is that good?" she breathed.

"I don't know. It's never happened with anyone else."

That was the first he'd admitted that she threw him for a loop, too. It was the first he'd admitted that he thought about kissing her when they weren't together. It was the first that Adam had given her hope that he still cared for her.

But then she remembered the letter that had blown into the corral—the letter that would make the next few years easier. She couldn't tell Adam about the scholarship…not here, not now, not when they were doing this. But she couldn't keep kissing him, either, going farther, knowing she'd leave him as she had the last time. He'd hate her if she did. She just knew he would.

Breathless, dizzy from desire, wishing everything was different, she rested her hands on his chest.

That was all it took for him to back away. "What's wrong?"

"I…you…your procedure—"

"Kissing seems to make everything else feel a lot better," he assured her with a sly smile.

She wished she could believe that. She wished she could believe an affair with Adam wouldn't hurt either of them, wouldn't leave them broken, wouldn't leave them resenting each other.

"I have to get supper started. I told Mom I'd drive in tonight and help her hang the pictures she found at a flea market."

Adam's gaze was penetrating as it studied her to see if she was lying. She wasn't, though the picture hanging could have waited till another night.

Dropping his hands to his sides, turning away toward the coffeemaker, he stated, "You should have just gone there straight from the hospital. It was silly to drive the whole way out here and then drive back in."

"I wanted to check on you."

His expression now was guarded. The coffeemaker began dripping as he turned to face her. "I told you before, Leigh, it was no big deal. I don't need a private nurse."

She knew he didn't want her professional concern, but it was all she could give him tonight. "Just because you don't want it, doesn't mean you don't need it."

The tension in the kitchen seemed to suck the air out of the room. The coffee dripped, dripped, dripped. The clock on the wall ticked, ticked, ticked. Her heart pounded as she read the desire in his eyes and felt it in her own body.

When the phone rang, she jumped.

Adam looked almost relieved as he said, "I'll get it."

Picking up the cordless phone on the counter, he greeted the caller.

When Leigh went to the refrigerator to pull out ingredients to start dinner, she heard Adam say, "I'm glad Sharon decided to come." There was a pause. "I'll think about that. I'll see you on Saturday."

After Adam returned the phone to its stand, Leigh could feel his gaze on her. She put the carrots on the counter. "That was your mother?" she guessed.

"Yes, she's getting married on Saturday at three. Sharon has promised to be there. Now all I have to do is figure out what to buy them as a wedding present."

As he reached for a coffee mug and poured a cup of coffee, Leigh realized Adam wasn't going to ask her to go with him. Since she'd backed away from him, he might have decided he didn't want her in his life.

What seemed best for both of them didn't seem right.

Could she live with that?

Chapter Twelve

On Friday after Leigh appreciatively sniffed the chili simmering in the slow cooker, she returned the lid to the crock. Before he left this morning, Adam had told her he'd be stopping to see Mark after work tonight. The chili would be ready whenever he got home.

Taking escarole and endive from the crisper drawer in the refrigerator to make a salad, she set them on the counter to prepare them for washing. She'd turned on the spigot when she remembered the load of laundry she still had to run through the dryer. She was trying to get the smell of smoke out of her clothes—the ones she'd salvaged, anyway.

She'd just turned off the spigot when the front door opened and Adam came in. One look at him told her his visit with Mark hadn't gone well. His shoulders were rigid, his jaw was set. There was a furrow across his brow that she suspected wasn't going to go away easily.

''How did it go?'' she asked gently, as she watched him come through the living room.

He was wearing a khaki-colored hooded jacket today. Shrugging out of it, he tossed it over the arm of the recliner. His tan oxford shirt, with its narrow navy stripe, was open at the collar. Adam's jeans fit Adam the way jeans should fit a man. And Leigh found her heart racing as he got closer—the way it always did.

His expression was somber. ''My God, Leigh. I didn't expect him to look so…so close to death. The last time I saw him he was pale and tired, but—'' He crossed to the dining area.

''He *was* near death, Adam, but he's coming back now. His body's fighting to make him well.'' Although Marietta had explained the process Mark would go through—the isolation, the special room—Leigh knew no one was really prepared to deal with it.

''I had to wear a mask and gloves and a gown. I felt as if I shouldn't be there…as if I were using the family's time.''

''You *are* family, Adam. You saved his life.''

''Not yet. If the transplant doesn't take, if he gets an infection—'' Adam rubbed the back of his neck ''—then there's no justice in this world. There's no fairness. It makes me wonder why we're here—''

She couldn't help but take Adam's hand. ''Look at the joy Mark has already brought into your life.''

Closing his eyes, Adam took a deep breath. "If he dies..."

Leigh had never been more aware of her deep feelings for Adam. Without hesitation she wrapped her arms around him and held on tight. He stiffened. But after a few seconds he enfolded her in his embrace, too. Their hearts beat in unison.

Adam still smelled of the outdoors. With his strength surrounding her, she could admit to herself how much she wanted him...had always wanted him. When she looked up at him, he gazed down at her with a hungry intensity that rocked her soul. There was a deeper need there, and male desire that wouldn't be eased with a few kisses.

As he dropped his arms, he said, "If I don't let you go now, we'll end up in my bedroom."

Although she released him, too, her eyes stayed on his. "Maybe it's time we gave into this. Maybe it's time we grab what we can now."

"You're not the type of woman who has an affair."

"No, I'm not. At least, not just with any man. But with you... I want to feel you again, Adam. I want to touch your skin and let you touch mine."

"Leigh."

His voice was a sharp warning, and she knew her words were as arousing as anything else they might do. Somehow she managed, "I've missed you, Adam." It had taken her this long to realize the emptiness inside of her had always been her loss of Adam. No other man had come close to filling up that space.

"If I touch you—" His hand stopped in midair.

"Touch me," she whispered.

Instead of touching her, he kissed her. His hand laced in her hair, holding her head, making sure she understood his need as his lips first took hers, and then his tongue invaded her mouth. Suddenly she understood the restraint and self-control he'd exhibited for the past few weeks, and she gave herself up to Adam's need, as well as her own. There was a depth to this kiss that she'd never felt from Adam before. She responded as she'd always wanted to respond—with her whole being.

They couldn't seem to get enough of each other. His hands pulled her T-shirt from her leggings as he kept kissing her. Through the sensual haze, she remembered she wanted to stroke him, too, and her fingers went to his shirt buttons. But their arms were getting all tangled up. They couldn't seem to keep kissing and get undressed, too.

Finally Adam swept her down the hall with him to his bedroom, kissing her the whole way. His bed was the closest piece of furniture. Somehow she found herself kneeling on the edge, staring up at him, unbuttoning his shirt.

Stilling her hands, he said, "Wait." Then he pulled her T-shirt up and over her head.

Adam's buttons took no time at all, but his expression told her he thought it took forever. When she finished, she moved her hands from his belt, up through the soft curly hair to his nipples.

When Adam groaned, she smiled.

"You're having too much fun." His voice was dark, husky, promising her the same fun she was giving him.

Reaching behind her, he unfastened her bra. Then with deliberate, studied slowness, he eased the straps down her arms, finally tossing the filmy fabric away. Taking her breasts into his hands, he let her nipples graze his palms. Then he did it again. Fireworks shot through her, sparking here, there and everywhere, causing small fires to light into a larger one that became her desire as well as Adam's. After he shrugged off his shirt, he sat down on the bed. Without warning, his lips surrounded her nipple. She thought she'd swoon from the pleasure of it.

His hands were tugging at her leggings and panties and soon she was lying on the bed, naked. She heard the clank of his belt buckle as he unfastened it, the rasp of his zipper as he skated it down. Then he was beside her, as naked as she was…as ready for their union as he had ever been. They needed to reaffirm life. They needed to know there was a reason for them being on this earth.

"Oh, Adam," she sighed, as she wrapped her hand around him, making him shudder with the intimate caress.

While they lay there face-to-face, Adam kissed her again, caressing her breasts, sliding his large hand down her hip, eventually slipping it between her thighs.

"Protection, Leigh. Are you on anything?"

"No. Do you have—"

Instead of answering her, he reached in the nightstand drawer, jerked it open and pulled out a foil packet. Then, apparently knowing what she was thinking and wondering, he admitted, "There have been a few women, Leigh. But I've always used protection. I've never taken any chances. Not with pregnancy. Not with anything else.''

If she could believe anyone in this world, it was Adam. Of course he'd had other women. Of course he'd gone on with his life.

At her silence, he tipped up her chin and looked into her eyes. ''We can still stop.''

She knew Adam *could* stop...*would* stop...because that was the kind of man he was. ''I don't want you to stop.''

''Those are golden words,'' he rasped close to her ear.

As he sucked her earlobe, she became so restless she couldn't keep still. Her hands searched his body for a place to land...a place to caress...a place to do to him what he was doing to her. They gave and took pleasure...gave and shared kisses...gave and caressed each other's bodies until they glistened with their desire.

When Adam tore open the foil packet, she asked, ''Can I do it?''

''You've grown bolder over the years,'' he teased with a smile.

''Maybe. Or maybe I know more about foreplay now.''

His eyebrows arched, and he laughed. ''From what you've read in books, of course.''

''Of course,'' she repeated so innocently that he had to kiss her before he let her apply the condom.

As she rolled the condom onto him with the teasing pleasure of a true courtesan, he sucked in a breath.

Then he took her hands, held them under his beside her head and muttered, ''Foreplay be damned.''

When Adam thrust into her, Leigh met his demand for satisfaction with a cry of pleasure. After that, she was sure she entered another realm. With each thrust she became more united with Adam. Her joy came from more than physical ecstasy, as he sent her spiraling from one peak to the next, each successively higher, each promising so much more. She teetered on the edge of erotic sensation for what seemed like forever, until suddenly she was climaxing, stars bursting all around her.

Adam cried his release.

Leigh loved Adam's weight on top of her...loved being able to nibble at his shoulder...loved licking the salt from his skin.

''Keep doing that, and we'll have to start all over,'' he mumbled into her neck.

''Would that be so bad?'' she asked, wondering if he now had regrets, wondering if he'd landed back on earth as fast as she had.

Where before Adam had been joking, now he raised himself on his elbows and said seriously, ''Not bad. But maybe not good for us, either. Maybe now we've gotten this out of our systems.''

His expression was unreadable and his guard was firmly back in place. She knew she had to be the one to take the risk. ''I don't think it's that simple. I'm not sure you and I could ever get enough.''

Adam's expression didn't change as he rolled onto his back, stared up at the ceiling, then pushed himself up and sat on the edge of the bed. "I'll be right back while you think about what tonight means."

As he disappeared into the bathroom, Leigh wondered just what he *was* thinking about. She found out when he returned a few minutes later.

Standing by the edge of the bed, he concluded, "We know where we stand this time, Leigh. We have a little over two months until you leave. It's up to us to decide what to do with it. Your plans haven't changed, have they?"

He was asking her if tonight had changed anything, and it had. It had made her aware of how serious she was about him. It had made her wonder if her dreams were *her* dreams or if they were her mother's. It had made her think about a medical degree and what that would mean for her future. "I received a full scholarship," she said softly. "That was the letter that blew into Thunder's corral."

Perfectly still, he looked away and then met her gaze again. "You're fortunate. Now you won't be in debt for years."

"I still have undergrad loans to pay. But it will make everything easier."

She could see he wouldn't ask her about the two of them. He wouldn't ask her to give up her plans. He wouldn't ask her to have an affair with him until she left. But that's what she was going to do.

Sitting up, she took in the taut muscles of Adam's shoulders, his washboard stomach, his tall, wonderfully built body. Just looking at him made her quiver inside, and she wasn't going to give this up. She wasn't going to give *him* up. Not yet.

Taking hold of all the courage she had ever possessed, all she might ever possess, she asked, ''Would you rather sleep alone, or would you like company?''

The green lights in his eyes told her what his answer would be before he said, ''I'd like the company, if *you're* the company.''

''I'm it.'' She tried to keep her voice light.

Lowering himself to the bed, he bent to kiss her.

Leigh let thoughts of the future and consequences burn away as their passion consumed them once more.

Pleased that Adam had asked her to go along to his mother's wedding, Leigh had dressed carefully, even though she knew the ceremony would be somewhat casual. She'd managed to salvage an emerald-green dress with a flared skirt and a short cropped jacket. After a few washings and a long ironing it looked good. Adam's expression when he saw her in it told her she'd chosen well.

The justice of the peace was located in a small house. John and Peggy had decided to get married in Portland, go out for a nice lunch afterward, then spend the night in a motel. Adam told her his mother hadn't stayed overnight anywhere—away from the farm—in years.

As the justice of the peace's wife introduced herself at the door, Leigh smiled and followed Chloe Wagner to a prettily decorated room with metal folding chairs and a white lectern. She couldn't help thinking about last night.

And this morning. She and Adam couldn't seem to get enough of each other. After they'd made love the first time, they'd done it again. Finally they'd eaten supper. But dessert had turned into desire and they'd gone back to bed. Eventually cuddling and falling asleep, they'd awakened hungry for each other again. Now whenever Adam looked at her, she knew what he was thinking. He was wishing they were back in bed. So was she.

After Mrs. Wagner left them in the wedding room, she went to answer the doorbell's peel.

Leigh asked Adam, "Are you sure your mom won't mind me coming?"

"I'm positive. She told me to bring a guest to make the occasion more festive. At the time I didn't think I would."

She knew what he meant. There had been so much tension between them before. After last night...

When Peggy Bartlett, soon to be Pavlichek, entered the small room with her fiancé and her daughter, Leigh recognized her immediately. The past ten years showed, but today, in her mauve suit, with an orchid corsage on her lapel and her wide smile, she looked as happy as any bride should look. When she saw Adam and Leigh, her green eyes opened wider.

She didn't hesitate to come toward them. "Leigh Peters?" she asked.

"Yes, ma'am. I hope you don't mind that Adam brought me along."

"Of course I don't mind." She motioned to her fiancé. "Come here, John. There's someone I want you to meet."

Sharon trailed behind the man who would soon be her stepfather. Leigh felt sorry for her. Adam had told

Leigh everything Sharon had said. His stepsister wasn't exactly frowning now, but she didn't look happy, either.

After introductions were made, Peggy turned to John. "Leigh and Adam were friends in high school. More than friends, I think." She sent Adam a knowing smile.

Before Adam could respond, John took him off the hook.

John Pavlichek was a big, burly man with a butterscotch shock of hair and a matching beard. Today he looked uncomfortable in his suit. But his tie was perfectly tied and his trousers meticulously creased. "That stove for your mother was a perfect wedding present. We couldn't have asked for anything nicer. She told me when we get back to the farm, she's going to start cooking up a storm."

Addressing Leigh, he explained, "It's one of those smooth-topped ranges. That oven's big enough for a twenty-pound turkey!"

Although she and Adam had discussed wedding presents briefly the night he'd received the call about the wedding, he hadn't told her what he'd decided. It seemed he'd chosen the perfect present, and a generous one, too. But she'd seen that generosity before—with Mark and with Shawna.

The justice of the peace entered then. He was a tall, thin man with almost no hair. After he made sure the paperwork was in order, he asked, "Shall we get started?"

As Sharon sat beside Leigh during the short ceremony, Leigh thought she saw a tear come to the woman's eyes when her mother made her promises. Leigh could only imagine what was going through her head.

Leigh had never known her own father. Honestly, she'd never wanted to know him, from what her mother had told her. Yet in many ways, she guessed he was like Jared Cambry. As a teenager he'd been afraid of responsibility, and he'd taken off for parts unknown rather than deal with the girl he had gotten pregnant and her unborn child. Years later her mother had heard through the grapevine that he'd been killed in a motorcycle accident. When Leigh learned of it, she had felt lost, even though the man had never been in her life. It was hard to imagine what losing a parent would actually be like.

Her mother had done so much for her over the years....

The vows Peggy and John took resonated with Leigh, and she could imagine saying them with Adam. She could actually see herself doing that. But as soon as the scene played in her mind, she switched it off. That wasn't where she and Adam were headed. His life was here in Portland, where he had grown a business, where he now had a family that seemed to become larger each day. She would be in Ohio. Long-distance relationships didn't work. She knew that. She also knew her hours would be long and not leave free time for even letter writing, let alone commutes home.

The ceremony ended and Mr. and Mrs. Wagner bestowed on the couple all of their good wishes. Leigh watched as Adam congratulated John and his mother.

It seemed there had been some healing there. At least, they all seemed at peace with the past.

Except for Sharon.

She was wearing tan slacks and an off-white blouse, and Leigh wanted to tell her she'd look so much more attractive in colors. Yet she knew the woman probably wouldn't listen or want anyone else's advice.

Adam made it clear that lunch after the ceremony was on him. He'd made reservations at one of Portland's finest restaurants, and Peggy's eyes glistened when he told her. "You didn't have to do that," she mumbled.

"I *wanted* to do that," Adam assured her.

A half hour later they were seated at a round table covered with a pale gray tablecloth. The silverware shone and the crystal sparkled.

They were eating their salads when Peggy asked Leigh, "Where do you work?"

"At Portland General. That's how Adam and I reconnected again...when he became the donor for Mark Cambry's transplant."

"There was an article in the paper about that yesterday," John reminded Peggy.

"Yes," she agreed. "Did you see it?"

Adam exchanged a glance with Leigh. With everything that was happening in their lives, she didn't think he'd even opened the paper in the past few days.

"I didn't see it," Adam admitted, and Leigh shook her head, indicating she hadn't, either. "Why would an article about that be in the paper?" he asked.

"Mr. Cambry is important in this community. And so are you. They talked about how Mr. Cambry's family wasn't a match. Then they wrote about you being his son. They quoted his daughter, Shawna, several times.''

''Maybe she picked up the phone when the reporter called,'' Leigh suggested, knowing how open Shawna was. ''I can't imagine Jared and Danielle giving out that information.'' She knew how Adam hated publicity, but this shouldn't affect him. His receptionist could always field calls he didn't want to handle.

''What work do you do at the hospital?'' Peggy asked, going back to her original question.

''I'm a nurse in the oncology unit. But that will be changing in June. I'll be attending med school.''

''Here?'' Peggy asked.

''No,'' Adam answered for her. ''In Ohio. She has a full scholarship. She has always dreamed of being a doctor, and now that dream is going to come true.''

He said it matter-of-factly, as if he were reminding himself of all of those facts. Although last night had been wonderful, although they'd talked about grabbing the moment and living in the present, she knew Adam. At some point he'd want to protect himself against the pain of her leaving. He'd shut down and close her out. She was sure of it.

''I'm going to be changing a few things in *my* life, too.'' Sharon had been quiet during lunch and it was the first time she had spoken.

''What kind of things?'' Adam asked, giving her his full attention.

''I applied for a promotion to manage the back claims department. I've been thinking about it for some time. I didn't really want to leave the group of people I'm working with in the intake division, but the salary's better. I'd also have another week's vacation."

"Those are advantages," Adam agreed. "Would you like the work as well as what you're doing now?"

"I think so. It would be less customer service, more of a supervisory position."

"When will you know if you got it?" Adam asked.

"I should know by the end of next week. But in the meantime—" she exchanged a glance with her mother "—I'm going to be looking at apartments."

"I told her she doesn't have to move out," Peggy said quietly.

"We've both told her that," John agreed, letting Adam know this wasn't his doing.

"Yes, you've both told me that," Sharon admitted. "But you two need your privacy. And I think it's time I...try living on my own." Then she gave Adam a glance that was a bit defiant but filled with pride, too.

After that, no controversial subjects arose. It was a pleasant lunch, and when Leigh and Adam drove back to the ranch, she thought he looked relieved.

"Your mom and John seemed pleased with the way the day went," Leigh commented. "They seem happy together."

"I wonder if they got married because it was practical for both of them. Mom is getting older and needs a man around the house. John... Well, he'll have the obvious advantages. Sex. Home-cooked meals."

"I think it's more than a practical marriage," Leigh protested. "I saw the way he looked at her, and the way she looked at him. I think they're really in love.

When John took her hands so gently in his, when he said his vows so fervently, it seemed he'd found someone he'd needed all his life. It's more than a practical arrangement,'' she said with certainty this time.

''You're a romantic,'' Adam said with a slight smile.

She'd never thought of herself in that way, but maybe she was.

As Adam drove up Cedar Run's lane to the house, they both spotted the silver sedan parked in the driveway.

''Are you expecting anyone?'' Leigh asked.

''No. I don't think it would be Lissa and Sullivan. They'd call before they drove up here.''

''Unless they wanted to surprise you.''

However, when Adam pulled up beside the car, they could see a man, a stranger, sitting inside.

Adam motioned to the man that he was going to pull into the garage and go around to the door. Then he pressed the remote.

A few minutes later Adam opened his front door. ''Can I help you?'' he asked the stranger.

Waiting near the sofa in the living room, Leigh wondered if this visitor could possibly be here for her. Not that she was expecting anyone, either.

The man was dressed in a button-down shirt and casual slacks. He was about five-eight, looked to be in his mid-thirties and kept pushing his glasses up higher on his nose. ''Adam Bartlett?'' he asked.

''Yes.''

''My name's Randy Seneft. I'm with *Breaking News* on the PQF network. Could we talk?''

After only a moment's hesitation, Adam stepped back and let the man inside.

Seneft glanced over at Leigh and then smiled at Adam. ''One of our producers saw the article in the paper yesterday...about you and Jared Cambry and the bone marrow transplant. We think it's a wonderful story and want to do a live interview as soon as possible. What do you say? Will you do the show live with us for millions of people to see?''

Chapter Thirteen

"I'm not doing a live interview. I'm not doing *any* kind of interview."

Leigh watched Adam's face harden as he realized exactly what the associate producer wanted.

On one hand, she knew Adam hated the idea of his life being opened for all to see. On the other, she knew the donor registry always needed publicity. The more people who signed up, the more lives could be saved. "You know, maybe you should hear him out," she suggested softly.

The bond that had been established between them last night seemed fragile now as his gaze met hers and she knew he wondered why she was even suggesting it.

"Yes, Mr. Bartlett, maybe you should hear me out.

Or at least hear what I'm proposing.'' The producer hurried on so Adam didn't have a chance to stop him. ''We'd like to do the interview at the hospital. I've already gotten Dr. Chambers's okay. We'll show a videotape of Mark—or run a local station's coverage of his soccer games, explaining his condition and what he's gone through. But the other aspect of this we'd like to explore is how Mr. Cambry found you, and of course your part in all this. I understand there was also a reunion with a twin sister, Lissa Cartright Grayson.''

''That's exactly what I don't want,'' Adam snapped. ''Being put on display for the public to see. Forget it, Mr. Seneft, I'm not interested.'' Adam opened the door wide so the man would leave.

As if he was playing his trump card, the producer stated, ''Mr. Cambry has already agreed to this interview and so has his family. They want to tell other parents that there's hope.''

''We don't even know if the transplant took yet,'' Adam said, clearly angry now.

''I understand that. But that's what makes this a good story. The public will follow it—follow Mark's progress.''

''And you don't give a hoot if everything turns out all right or not. You don't care if Mark lives or dies, as long as you get ratings.''

The producer shook his head. ''Ah, Mr. Bartlett. You want to think the media is made up of heartless souls who are only interested in the story and the public's response to it. That's simply not true. Of course we care. We want Mark to make it. And think of all the people he'll have praying for him.''

"That's low," Adam growled. "If you and the Cambrys want to do the story, that's fine. But I won't have any part of it."

Quickly, before Adam could push him out the door, Mr. Seneft took a card from his pocket and shoved it into Adam's hand. "I realize the idea of an interview has all come as a surprise to you, but I want you to think this over. We're planning the taping for Tuesday night. All you have to do is give me a call to tell me if you want to join us."

Adam remained stonily silent.

"Mr. Bartlett, I really think this would just make a heartwarming story. You trying to save a little boy's life. A family reunited. Please think about it."

After a last look at Adam's set expression, the producer turned and left.

As Leigh sat down on the sofa, she could hear the producer drive away. There was so much she wanted to say, yet this was Adam's decision. He had his reasons for wanting to keep his life private. Still…

He was studying her now. After a last look to make sure Seneft was gone, he crossed the room. "Say what you have to say, Leigh. I know there's something on your mind."

Ever since they first met, Adam could read her. Sometimes that was unsettling. When she searched for the right words to use, he shook his head. "Just say it, Leigh. You're talking to me, not one of your patients."

Tact was a part of her profession, and she realized now he didn't want that. He wanted honesty. "All right. I think this is your chance to foster the donor transplant registry. To get the word out. To bring people in. You're giving up the opportunity before you even look at what it could do.''

As he shook his head, he lowered himself to the sofa on the cushion beside her. ''I don't want my life laid out for everybody to see. I don't want to have to relive it. I know exactly what will happen if I agree to this. It won't be the cut-and-dried human interest story that producer says it will be. They'll sensationalize everything. They'll cut and paste and edit until it looks exactly like they *want* it to look.''

''Do you watch *Breaking News?*''

''No. I've never seen it. I don't have much time or taste for network TV, for the reasons I just told you.''

''*Breaking News* isn't like some of the other news segment programs. It's in very good taste. I read an article in the Sunday paper on how they put the show together. They look for good, human-interest stories that don't make national news, but yet carry a load of impact for the viewing public. They focus on the lives of whomever's involved, and how the event or the situation has impacted them. It's about people more than about the story. I'm sure both you and Jared would have a say in where you want the focus.''

Adam stared at the dark screen of the television, as if he was imagining all of it on there, and he didn't like any of what he saw. ''Publicity can so easily get out of hand. It's the last thing I want. Even when Novel Programs, Unlimited's, stock went public, I stayed in the background and let Dylan lead the parade. I did it for a very good reason. I didn't want reporters poking into my life. They'll bother Mom and

John. They might even dig up something on Owen. No one wants to be exposed. I just don't like the whole idea of it. You're the one who wants to save lives. Sometimes I just want to go back to the way my life was before all of this started."

There was an underlying message in Adam's tone. The past month had caused nothing but upheaval in his life, and he didn't like it. Although he might be grateful Shawna and Mark were in his life now, and Lissa too, he didn't know where any of it was going to lead. Jared hadn't welcomed him as a son into his family with open arms, and since the transplant was over and done, Adam might feel as if he were no longer necessary.

Resurrecting the relationship she and Adam once had and getting involved again hadn't been wise on either of their parts, and yet she didn't regret it. Maybe *he* did.

"Are you sorry I became your liaison? Are you sorry last night happened?"

"Last night happened because we decided to give in to the chemistry between us, and later be damned. But later's going to come, Leigh. I know it, and you know it. If you thought writing me that note was tough, imagine how you're going to feel when you take off for Cleveland."

Pushing himself up from the sofa, he added, "Or maybe it won't be any more difficult than the last time. Maybe you let last night happen because you knew that."

Her heart ached because he was implying she didn't care as much as he did. He was implying that an affair was easy for her, that it wasn't going to tear her apart when they had to say goodbye. She couldn't even find the words to respond. She found all of her feelings were clogging her throat, and she couldn't get even one of them out.

When he rose to his feet, he avoided her gaze. ''I'm going to change and then take Thunder for a ride. Rain is rolling in again tonight and I want to take him for a good workout.''

She just nodded, overwhelmed with the enormity of leaving Adam again...overwhelmed with the enormity of chasing a dream that she wasn't sure was hers anymore.

The guard in the lobby of the building where Novel Programs, Unlimited, was located nodded to Adam as he let the glass doors shut behind him on the following afternoon. The overcast, gray sky outside fit Adam's mood. Ever since that producer had turned up on his doorstep last night...

Tony Pasqual, sitting behind his desk in his security uniform, gave Adam a wide-toothed grin. ''This is a busy place for a Sunday.''

That wasn't what Adam wanted to hear. The tension between him and Leigh since their discussion last night hadn't abated. She'd slept in the guest room. That wasn't what he'd wanted. But after their conversation last evening, his pride had kept him silent when she'd told him that's what she was going to do. Their night in bed together had been a denial of reality. Grabbing the moment in the dark of night had seemed like a good philosophy…until they'd looked at it in the light of day.

Do you really want to go back to life as you knew it before Jared's visit? he asked himself.

He'd meant every word he'd said to her last night. Looking at Leigh, the twist of the knife in his gut when he thought about her leaving, had pushed him to answer her as he had. This morning after a ride on Thunder that hadn't helped at all, after Leigh had made brunch and they'd forced conversation, after thinking about Mark isolated in that sterile hospital atmosphere, Adam had decided work would be his salvation today.

But he'd wanted to work alone, and he hoped anybody else Tony had signed in was working on another floor.

The guard turned the log book to face Adam.

Picking up the pen, Adam scrawled his name, the date and the time, seeing that Dylan and Darlene were signed in before him. Terrific.

"So you've had traffic already today?" he asked.

"You could say that. On your floor, anyway. Mr. Montgomery and Miss Allen said that they had correspondence to catch up on that had backed up last week."

Dylan had flown to Chicago earlier in the week and had been tied up in meetings at the end of it. Apparently, he'd enlisted Darlene's help in catching up.

As Adam took the elevator to the fifteenth floor, he realized he hadn't helped Dylan with his problem with Darlene. On the other hand, Adam didn't know what he could do. He wasn't having a problem with his secretary, Dylan was. It had been more than three weeks since his partner had voiced his concerns. Maybe the whole thing had blown over, or Dylan had brought it out into the open.

Bringing everything out into the open wasn't always the best idea, either. Look at what happened when he and Leigh had finally admitted and acted on what was going on between them. Last night Adam's bed had never felt more empty. Last night he'd wished the past had stayed in the past—along with his desire for Leigh.

Fluorescent lights buzzed overhead, shedding their white glow into the hall as Adam stepped from the elevator. The sky looked even grayer out of the windows up here. He wished he'd put Thunder into his stall instead of leaving him in the corral.

Adam stopped for a moment before the glass doors stenciled with Novel Programs, Unlimited's, bold lettering and logo. He had made his work his life until the past few weeks. Hadn't his course been a lot less bumpy that way?

When he stepped into the wine, cream and black reception area, he wasn't surprised not to find Darlene at her desk. If she and Dylan were going over the minutes of last week's meetings and connected paperwork, they'd be in Dylan's office. Better to stop in and make conversation now, rather than to get interrupted later. Once he closed his office door, he didn't want to be disturbed.

The wine-and-black tweed carpeting muffled his footsteps as he made his way to Dylan's office. He heard the sound of Darlene's light laughter, the baritone of Dylan's voice. But as he came to Dylan's office and pushed open the ajar door, he felt like an intruder into a Sunday-afternoon matinee. Dylan was in his office, but he wasn't working. He was sitting in his oversized leather chair with Darlene on his lap! Darlene's hair was mussed, her lipstick smeared, and the buttons of her blouse were open. They both started like guilty teenagers when they saw him.

Adam could have backed out. He could have mumbled an excuse and left. He could have pretended he didn't see what he saw. But he liked Darlene. She was a good secretary, and he didn't want to lose her. If Dylan was just fooling around…

"Have I interrupted something?" he asked, with the nonchalance that widened both pairs of eyes that were on him.

As Darlene tried to scramble away from Dylan's lap, the CFO kept her still. "Don't go anywhere," he mumbled to her as he pulled her blouse together and held the material in his fist. "Adam, if you could give us a minute," Dylan said in a patient tone.

"I think you need more than a minute for what you were into. At least I *hope* so."

A dark flush crept up Dylan's neck. "This isn't what you think."

Now Darlene managed to hike herself off Dylan's lap, quickly buttoned the buttons of her yellow cotton shirt, then shakily ran a hand through her brown hair. Her face had paled.

Squaring her shoulders, she said to Adam, "Mr. Bartlett, I…I'm sorry you found me in this unprofessional…position. I like working for you, and I promise if you keep me on, it won't happen again."

Dylan was out of his chair in a shot. "What do you mean it won't happen again? We're dating. Of course it's going to happen again."

Adam had never seen his friend quite so rattled. "Darlene, this is Sunday. Your time's your own. I'm not going to fire you. But maybe you could give me a few minutes with Dylan?"

Avoiding Adam's gaze, as well as Dylan's, she skittered to the door. "I'll be out at my desk."

"Darlene," Dylan commanded, as if he didn't want her to leave.

She said again, "I'll be at my desk."

The silence that enveloped the office had never been quite so tense between the two friends. Finally Adam broke it. "Do you think that's wise?"

"Don't act like a big brother," Dylan muttered. "And don't talk to me about wise, when you have your high school sweetheart living at the ranch and you know she'll be history again in a couple of months."

Uh-oh. Dylan was on the offensive. For a guy who was usually placid, he seemed undeniably unnerved. Adam didn't take the bait. "Darlene's a nice woman, Dylan. I'd hate to see her get hurt. She's the one who might be too uncomfortable staying here if you decide Natalie fits your lifestyle better."

"Natalie's gone. She and I were never…compatible."

"And you and Darlene are?"

"It might not look like it, but yes, we are. We both went to parochial school."

Adam raised a brow.

Dylan's hand slashed through the air defensively. "It impacted her more than it impacted me, but the point is we have similar backgrounds. She has as much energy as I do. She's a night owl who can get up at 5:00 a.m. if she has to. She's terrific fun. When I talked to her about the letters, she offered to resign. You were right. She was having a problem with them because she was trying to make them perfect. She admitted she liked me."

Adam smiled at the surprise in Dylan's voice. "You're a likeable guy."

Dylan shook his head. "I mean it, Adam. She likes me for me, not because I'm CFO of this company, not because I drive a Jaguar, and not because I can fly her to Hawaii for the weekend and the cost won't dent my bank account. We've seen each other almost every night for the past week, and all she wants to do is cuddle in front of the TV and eat popcorn with me."

Adam gave Dylan a skeptical look.

"As opposed to having dinner in a five-star restaurant," Dylan explained. "That's what I like about her. No pretense. No edge. And I find that I like staying in with her."

That statement, above all others, impacted Adam. He knew Darlene was a sincere, honest, hardworking young woman. It seemed as if she'd gotten to his partner in a big way.

"Are you telling me this is serious?"

"More serious than *I've* ever been."

"Maybe she should just work as *my* secretary and

you should hire another one. Then, if things don't work out, it might not be so awkward."

"I'd rather keep her as *our* secretary and think that things *will* work out. Where's your optimism, Adam?"

Adam looked away from his friend and out into the gray sky. "My optimism is in a nosedive right now."

"Things not working out with trying to be 'just friends' with the former lover?"

Dylan was entirely too perceptive. Adam wasn't about to spill his guts, or admit how unsettled he was about Leigh and everything else that had happened. "This is where I leave." He moved toward the door.

"You can poke into my life, but I can't poke into yours?"

"That sounds like a good policy," Adam joked.

Dylan shook his head. "One of these days, you're going to realize that all of those safety fences you've built around yourself don't do one bit of good. They might keep people out, but they don't prevent you from feeling what goes on inside."

"You've missed your calling. You should host a talk show."

"And you, my friend, need to get honest with yourself."

Unsure of exactly what Dylan meant, Adam didn't respond. He left Dylan's office, crossed to his and shut the door. The computer beckoned to him, and he liked the familiarity of it. Right now, he liked the idea of losing himself in cyberspace and shutting everything else out.

If Adam thought he could lose himself in cyberspace, three hours later he knew he couldn't. He'd skipped from one project to another all afternoon. None of them kept his attention for very long. All of his thoughts kept coming back to Leigh and Mark and Jared Cambry.

Dylan had stopped in an hour ago and said he and Darlene were leaving. Now, in the silent office building, Adam heard a sound that was unusual for this time of year. The grumble of thunder. Rain was part and parcel of Portland's charm. Once in a while, storms rolled in from the mountains, but that was rare for the end of March. Weather patterns had seemed to change over the past few years, though.

Staring out the window, he thought he saw a flash of lightning. Damn! And Thunder was out in the corral. He didn't like the idea of the horse getting spooked. With the door of his stall open, he could go inside. But *would* he?

Adam shook his head. Sometimes animals didn't know what was good for them any better than humans did.

What was good for *him?* Adam wondered. He simply didn't know anymore.

Fifteen minutes later, flashes of lightning occurred more often as Adam drove home, his foot heavy on the accelerator. Darkness had fallen, and rain was pouring down by the time he had parked in the garage. Lights were turned on in the house, but he couldn't find Leigh anywhere. Lightning cracked, sounding as if it had hit something close by, then thunder rolled over the dining room skylight, threatening and loud. Leigh's car was in the driveway. Going to the foyer closet, he found her jacket missing. She wouldn't have gone to the barn. She wouldn't have…

Without even thinking about stopping to grab his coat, Adam raced outside, across the yard and lane to the corral. He couldn't believe his eyes. Under the forceful white glare of the barn's floodlight, he could see Leigh had her hood up, buttoned around her face, and was carrying a lead rope in her hand as she made her way toward Thunder. The stallion stood at the far end of the corral under the shelter of two maple trees. Before Adam could move, Leigh was hurrying across the corral. All he could think about was the day Delia had opened the gate…had stepped inside—

Lightning seemed to strike a nearby fence. Great rolls of thunder boomed as Leigh approached the horse. Thunder reared up, and Adam was moving over the fence in a leap, then proceeding at a dead run across the corral. Lightning flashed as Adam relived the day when he was seven—every emotion, every fear, every regret. The memories seemed so terrifyingly real that when he peered through the rain and saw Leigh was out of harm's way, he almost couldn't believe it.

Thunder reared up again, and Adam was afraid she wouldn't be as lucky the second time…afraid he couldn't reach her before the unthinkable happened.

Unaware of anything but what she was doing, Leigh waited until Thunder was on all four hooves again, then she grabbed his halter, hooking on the lead.

Her hood slipped from her head, and rain washed down over her hair as lightning lit up the sky a third time.

Adam reached her and yanked the lead rope from her hand. ''What the hell are you doing out here?'' he yelled. ''Get into the barn. Get away from a horse that could trample you down with one hoof.''

''I couldn't leave him out here.''

''Get into the barn!'' he commanded again and waited until she ran toward the shelter. Then he patted Thunder's neck and ran with the horse into his stall.

Leigh was standing on the inside walkway, and Adam didn't say a word as he unhooked the lead, closed the outside stall entrance and climbed over the fence, landing beside her. Adrenaline was still rushing through him, hard and fast.

He was so furious with her, language didn't come easily. ''You could have been killed.'' The words sounded gritty and harsh. He was soaked and she wasn't much better, but he didn't care about that right now.

''I know how much he means to you,'' she said, her eyes huge. ''I didn't want anything to happen to him. When the storm turned severe, I didn't know what to do. I didn't know when you'd be home because you didn't tell me. You didn't call.''

He hadn't told her because he hadn't known. He hadn't called because he hadn't known what to say to her. Now all he could say again was, ''You could have gotten yourself killed.''

Swiping drops of rain from her face, she looked angry, too, as she returned, ''People who care do things because they're right, no matter what the risk.''

''Do what's right? You don't want to do what's right, Leigh. You want to do what's convenient. You don't want to do what's right, you want to hang on to a dream that's as old as you are. Is *that* right?''

She took a shaky breath. ''It is for *me.* Don't you see this is exactly what I was trying to avoid ten years ago when I wrote you that note? Don't you see it would have been that much harder if we had stayed together?''

''So you took the easy way out? No courage or risk there.'' He shook his head, knowing what he had to say, but not wanting to say it. He didn't want her to leave, but she was going to go anyway. ''You're the one who broke us apart once before, and you're the one who's going to do it again. So maybe we should both take the easy way out. We might as well just end this now.''

He spotted the quick glitter of tears before Leigh turned away. He saw the quiver of her chin right before she ran out of the barn.

But he didn't go after her. There was no reason to. She had made up her mind ten years ago, and he was old news. *They* were old news.

Going to the tack room, he picked up a towel to wipe down Thunder, denying the pain in his heart, the tightness in his throat and the burning behind his eyes.

Chapter Fourteen

It was seven o'clock Monday morning when the phone rang. Leigh was getting dressed, trying to find something in her suitcase on the sofa that didn't need to be ironed. Since her mother was in the shower, she ran for the phone in the kitchen, using every bit of energy she had. She hadn't slept all night. She missed Adam more than she could say. Everything that had happened with Thunder and afterward had plagued her throughout the night as she'd rolled it all over in her head.

Now she tried to shake herself awake as she picked up the phone, hoping desperately it was Adam. Maybe they could work things out. Maybe she could fly to Portland and he could fly to Cleveland. Maybe the hours wouldn't be as grueling as she imagined. Maybe—

The phone rang insistently again and she picked it up. "Hello."

"Miss Peters? It's Jared Cambry."

She tried to find her professional voice. "Hello, Mr. Cambry."

"I didn't know if you'd be at this number or not. I couldn't reach either of the numbers you gave me, and when I called information, they listed this one for your mother."

"Yes, I'm sorry I didn't call you with the new number. There was a fire at our apartment and I…I was staying somewhere else for a while. I lost my cell phone in the fire and haven't gotten another one yet. What can I do for you?"

"I have a request. I was speaking to Mr. Seneft, the producer for *Breaking News.* He told me he spoke to you and Adam."

"Yes, he did. Adam turned down the interview."

"Yes, I know that. This morning I'm going to try to convince him to change his mind. But even if he doesn't, I'd like you to take part. Marietta Watson will be away next week. She won't be able to explain the transplant process on air. We'd also like to promote the donor registry. You're knowledgeable about both of those things. I wondered if you'd consider doing the interview."

"Adam was concerned everything would be sensationalized."

"I know. The producer told me that. But I have Seneft's guarantee that everything will go exactly as we script it. This won't be tabloid news, Miss Peters. You'll have a real chance to get the word out about the good work that's being done. What do you say?''

''Do you think you can convince Adam to do the interview?''

There was silence on the other end of the line for a few seconds. ''I don't know. I haven't handled very well anything else where he's concerned lately.''

''You've been worried about Mark.''

''Yes, I have. But Danielle pointed out a few things to me, and I'm going to see Adam this morning. Will you do the interview even if he doesn't?''

She thought about her work in oncology…the children and what she believed in. ''Yes, I'll do it. Just tell me where and when.''

A few minutes later when she hung up the phone, her mother came out of the bedroom, dressed for her day. ''Before you go to Cleveland, you should think about buying a couple of suits on sale. They're professional, and you might need them. I've also gotten a box together of spare products—shampoos, lotions, that kind of thing.''

When she'd come home last night with her suitcase, Leigh's mother hadn't said a word. She'd accepted her back as if it had been inevitable. Adam's name hadn't been spoken. Now Leigh knew it had to be. In fact—

Ever since she'd moved into her new apartment, her mother had been planning and buying and worrying about everything Leigh should take to Cleveland…about her schedule when she was there…about her trip home over the Christmas holidays if she could get away. For the past few weeks as well as most of the night, Leigh had thought about the differences between being a nurse and a doctor. She'd thought about how these days doctors had little time with their patients. What she enjoyed most was working with patients—comforting them, informing them, being a friend to them. The more she'd thought about what Adam had said, about her dream being as old as she was, about becoming a doctor being an ambition of her mother's, all of it had rung true.

She'd admitted to herself she was falling in love with Adam again. What she hadn't admitted was that ten years ago she had loved him, and she loved him still.

Was accepting the scholarship and becoming a doctor the easy way out? It had seemed ludicrous. Yet it made sense, too. Why couldn't she trade one dream for another? Why couldn't she do the work she loved and have a life with Adam? Maybe he wouldn't still want her. Maybe she'd destroyed their chance to have a future by turning her back on him again.

"Leigh? Did you hear what I said?"

"About the lotion and the shampoo?"

"No. About the suits. Ever since last night you've been so distracted. Who was that on the phone so early? Was it Adam?"

Her mother sounded horrified at the thought, and Leigh had to put a stop to that. She had to put a stop to a lot of things.

"No. It was Jared Cambry. *Breaking News* is going to do a story about his family and finding Adam and the transplant. He wants me to be part of the interview."

"Do you think it's wise to get involved with a TV production?"

Taking a deep breath, Leigh said, "I'm going to do it because Jared Cambry's story is an important one. It will give me a chance to talk about the transplant program."

"Well, if you think that's best. I suppose Adam will be a part of this interview?"

"I'm not sure he *will* be. I'm hoping he will because I have a few things I need to tell him. I left Cedar Run last night when I shouldn't have. We had an argument—"

"About what? Did he ask you to stay here? Did he ask you to give up your scholarship?"

"No, Mom, he didn't. And now I realize why. He wants my dreams to be my *own* dreams. He doesn't want to interfere with what *I* really want. Just like *I* haven't interfered with what *you* really want."

"I don't know what you mean."

"Ten years ago Adam and I *were* young. I accepted your advice and your guidance. Maybe I didn't know what I truly wanted then. Or maybe romance looked bigger than life. But you got through to me, and I broke up with him. Now I know I shouldn't have."

Claire looked shocked. "Of course you should have. You're a nurse now, and on your way."

"Yes, I'm a nurse. And even if Adam and I had stayed together, I think I still would have become a nurse. I love my work. I want to care for kids with cancer every day, not spend more years of my life in school. Most of all, I love Adam. I'm not going to leave Portland, Mom. I'm not going to med school."

Though her mother's face had paled and Claire sank down on one of the thrift-store chairs, Leigh went on as kindly as she could. "I know how you've sacrificed for me. I know how you've worked for me. I appreciate all of it. But I'd be doing both of us an injustice if I went to med school because it was *your* dream."

"You could become an oncology specialist and help so many patients."

"I can help patients now...in a different way."

"What did he say to you last night? What did he do?"

"He told me the truth, Mom. He was honest with me. Now I can be honest with myself." Crossing to her mother, Leigh knelt down beside the chair. "Even if Adam won't take me back, even if I can't convince him that we can have a future together, I'm going to stay here. It's what I want to do. Will you accept that? Can you support my decision?"

At first Claire looked as if she were about to protest, about to give a laundry list of reasons why Leigh was throwing her life away. But then she looked into her daughter's eyes. "I guess if your feelings for Adam Bartlett have lasted all these years, there must be something to them."

"And you can still be proud of me if I stay in nursing and forget about med school?"

"If that's what you really want, honey, I'm not going to stand in your way. I don't want to lose you. You're all I have."

"Maybe. Maybe soon you'll have Adam, too."

When her mother didn't look convinced about that, Leigh smiled. Tonight she'd call Mr. Cambry and find out if Adam was going to do the interview. If he was, she'd find a way to tell him everything that was in her heart and hope that he would accept her love.

When Darlene buzzed Adam that Jared was in the reception area, he closed the catalog on his desk. "Send him back."

Did this personal visit mean that Mark was worse? That the transplant wasn't going to take?

Adam was on his feet when Jared entered the office, and his worry must have shown because Jared quickly said, "It's not Mark. I'm not here because of Mark."

There was great seriousness behind Jared's statement, and Adam looked at him curiously. "Why are you here?"

Jared didn't sit down, but crossed to the credenza, picked up the replica of a Model-T Ford, glanced at the Mustang next to it, then took a deep breath and faced his son. "Danni gave me hell after Shawna's party."

"About what?" He knew Danielle could be fiercely protective of her children, but her giving Jared hell painted quite a picture.

"She didn't like the way I introduced you at the party."

Adam remained silent.

"The truth is, I wanted to introduce you as my son, but I didn't know how you'd feel about that. I haven't known what to do about you...and Lissa. I think she and I are finding our way. But *you* and I...maybe it's harder because you *are* a son. Maybe it's harder because I think we're a lot alike."

Jared held up his hand right away. ''Oh, I don't mean in the way we've handled our lives. I certainly did a poor job of that at the beginning. But neither of us has said very much about all of this. *I* should have. It was my place. You were my son. Yes, you might have saved Mark's life, and I will appreciate that to my dying day. But you are a gift, too, Adam. A gift I didn't deserve. A gift maybe I still don't deserve.'' He looked lost for a moment. ''I'm saying this all badly.''

''No. No, you're not. I mean...you're right. Neither of us knew how to handle this. It seems you've been uncertain in how to react to me, and I was unable to reach out to you. I would have been terrifically proud if you had introduced me as your son.''

Adam could see the same emotion *he* felt in his father's eyes. Jared tried to speak and couldn't. Instead he reached out to Adam. ''From now on, everyone I meet will know you're my son.''

Adam wasn't sure exactly how it had happened, who had taken the first step, but suddenly they were embracing. And, in an odd way, Adam felt as if he'd found a home.

Obviously embarrassed by emotion he wasn't used to exhibiting, Jared released Adam, backed up a few steps and cleared his throat. ''I know you told the producer of *Breaking News* you didn't want to be interviewed, but I'd like you to reconsider. You're a member of my family, and I want you to be a part of this.''

Because Adam hadn't been able to reach out to his father, today might never have happened. Jared had taken the first step, and Adam saw now that he needed to reconsider a lot of things. He hadn't reached out to Leigh, either. He hadn't admitted that he…loved her. The quiet truth had been there all along; he just hadn't been silent enough to hear it. He'd thought the feelings belonged to long ago. They didn't. They belonged to now. If he had told her he loved her…if he had told her he wanted to make their relationship work…

What was he willing to give up?

He had enough money in his investments and in the bank that he could retire anytime he wanted. He could leave Portland and start up a new firm in Cleveland. They *could* be together, if that's what she really wanted, too. Last night he'd thought only his bed was empty. That was simply the tip of the iceberg. His life was empty without her.

"I'll do the interview if we can sign Leigh on, too. Is that possible?"

His father's smile was knowing as he confessed, "I already did that this morning."

As Leigh entered the lounge on the third floor of Portland General, cameras seemed to be everywhere. So did cords and lights, technicians and microphones. When she'd called Jared last night, he'd told her Adam would be here.

She saw the sofa and chair lined up on the makeshift stage. She saw the other chair and cameras set up for single interviews. Then she saw Adam in a suit and tie, talking to the producer, looking as serious as he had ever looked. She absolutely couldn't go through this taping without talking to him first. She thought she could, but now, seeing him—

They still had a half hour until airtime, and before she could change her mind, she marched over to him and said, ''Excuse me?''

The producer gave her an odd look. ''I need to give Adam some last-minute instructions, and then it will be your turn.''

''I'm sorry, but I need to talk to Adam for a few minutes first.'' Looking straight into Adam's eyes she said, ''It's not about Mark. It's about us.''

Adam's green eyes seemed to go a shade darker as the producer glanced from him to Leigh and back to Adam again. Checking his watch, he said tersely, ''Five minutes. You have five minutes.''

Intending to not waste a moment of that time, she asked, ''Will you come with me?''

She half expected him to say no. She half expected him to put her off until after the taping. He was a business-first kind of guy.

Instead of commenting, or answering her, he moved out in front of her and broke a direct path through everyone milling about into the hall. Once there, he glanced down the corridor, apparently finding what he was looking for. ''Down here.''

She followed him, not caring where they went, eager to tell him what she had to say, desperate to find out if he was going to give her a chance.

To her surprise, he opened the door to a broom closet. It took her back to her high school days, and she hoped this was a good omen. He switched on the light, and after they were both inside, he closed the door.

''I'm not going to medical school,'' she blurted out.

"I'm not going to Cleveland. I'm staying here. I love you, Adam. I hope I haven't realized how much too late. I just want to keep being a nurse, working with kids and live in Portland with you."

During the moments he didn't speak, tears came to her eyes, and she thought she'd never breathe again. But then he was holding her shoulders, bringing her closer. "You can't give up your dream for me."

"I'm not giving it up for you. I'm just changing dreams, to one of a life for *us*."

"You beat me to the punch," he said with a tender smile that made her heart soar. "I was going to move to Cleveland because I love you and I know we can make anything work. Anything," he insisted, as he tipped her head up and found her lips with his.

Adam's kiss was long and slow and deep. She'd never felt the depth and fervor of his emotion quite like this before. She responded the only way she could—with everything she was and everything she wanted to give him. There was so much more than desire. There were memories and forgiveness and hope and promise.

Reluctantly, it seemed, he broke away, tipped his head against hers and then leaned back. "I've been doing a lot of thinking."

"There's a lot of that going around," she confessed, trying to lighten the mood a little.

He traced his thumb along her cheek. "I love you, Leigh. More than anything else, I want you to be happy."

"I *will* be happy…with you."

"I've been holding back too much. Giving too little.

Not reaching out when I could. That's been brought home to me so many ways in the past month. When I was going over all the scenarios in my head of what could happen today, I had already made a decision about something I wanted to do with Cedar Run Ranch, whether I stayed here or went to Cleveland with you.''

''You don't want to keep it?''

''Oh, yes, I want to keep it. But if I couldn't be here, I was going to hire someone good to run it. However, since you've decided to stay in nursing, would you consider a different kind of work?''

''What work?'' He had her intrigued now.

''What if we turn the ranch into a camp for kids with cancer? You could be the director of the program and the on-site nurse. I could manage the logistics and financial details.''

''What about Novel Programs, Unlimited?''

''Dylan can run it. It can practically run by itself, anyway. I can keep my hand in if I want to. But most of my time would be devoted to Cedar Run.''

''I absolutely *love* the idea. I have so many contacts—in oncology and physical therapy...and in counseling, too.''

''Anybody but that Reed character you saw at the zoo.''

''Were you jealous?''

''Who? Me? Not any more than you were of Nicole.''

''I was not—''

''The truth. Always the truth.''

He was right. If she had been completely honest

with herself about all of this, about her life and everything she was feeling, they wouldn't have had to go through another difficult parting. "I *was* jealous, Adam. And I'm sorry. I'm sorry for everything I've put us through."

This time his finger covered her lips. Then his lips covered her mouth again, and she knew he'd forgiven her for all of it...because he loved her. Her love for him had lasted all these years. Now she knew it would last until the end of time.

Epilogue

The beginning of April in Portland was often as rainy as March. But today the sun was shining as Adam and Dylan entered Cedar Run Ranch's spare barn in tuxedos.

In just a week Adam had hired a decorator to transform the empty space into a wedding chapel. As Adam's gaze canvassed the barn, he couldn't believe what had been accomplished. Rows of white wooden chairs were filled with his and Leigh's wedding guests—everyone from Jared, Danielle, Shawna and Chad, to Peggy and John and Sharon and Claire. Lissa and Sullivan also sat with them. Adam couldn't believe that not only were all these people his family, but they *felt* like family now—even Sharon, who had grudgingly admitted she'd like to attend. Dylan was his best man, and Adam had also invited Darlene—who still seemed to ''like'' Dylan—as well as employees he valued and Leigh's friends and co-workers.

There were flowers everywhere—white gladiolus, white roses, white daisies. But the most beautiful scent emanated from the gardenia arbor.

The harpist began playing as Adam and Dylan walked up the center aisle to stand by the minister. There was only one person missing today, and that was Mark. They were all still praying for him, hoping with him. The whole country was doing that now. Their interview about the transplant and Lissa and Adam's reunion had caught fire, and they had also all been interviewed on the morning news. In addition, another segment show had aired clips. The whole country was sending their prayers skyward for Mark, and that couldn't do anything but help.

Dylan winked at Adam as they turned to face the back of the barn.

The wedding planner, a woman in her midforties who had been doing this for years, rolled the white runner up the center aisle.

The harp music changed.

Adam felt as if he'd waited for this moment all of his life. As soon as he saw a flurry of white, a bit of lace, his head came up and his gaze sought Leigh.

She looked like a princess. The gown was lace and pearls, full and billowing. She'd told him the train seemed to stretch for miles. He didn't care about that.

He only cared about her. She wore the pearl necklace her mother had given her for graduation. Somehow it had survived the fire and the cleanup. Her hair was arranged on top of her head, and the veil framed her face like a waterfall. Step by step, she moved closer to him, and it was hard to take his eyes from her face. But he wanted to take in all of her. A bouquet of white roses cascaded from her hands.

And then he saw it. Something that seemed out of place. On her wrist…

The tightness in his chest blurred his eyes for a moment as he realized she was wearing the bracelet he'd bought her ten long years ago. She'd kept it all this time. She'd loved him all this time.

When Leigh reached the arbor, Dylan had already stepped aside. Her mother, her matron of honor, took her bouquet, kissed her on the cheek and smiled at Adam. They'd form a friendship eventually, he and Claire. It had already started. Since he was taking care of the wedding, she had insisted on having a dinner for him and his family last night. She'd rented a room in a restaurant and all of it had gone better than Adam could ever have imagined. Everyone had mingled and talked and joked. At the end of the evening, he'd hugged his soon-to-be mother-in-law.

Taking Leigh's hands, he couldn't imagine ever letting her go. They'd decided they wanted a traditional ceremony with traditional vows. Now as he promised to love and cherish Leigh forever, he understood exactly what that meant. She understood, too, as she squeezed his hands, gazed into his eyes and smiled so tremulously. He wanted to kiss her right then.

The ceremony seemed to be over in a wink, and soon they faced friends and family as Mr. and Mrs. Adam Bartlett.

Pulling strings, Adam had managed on short notice to reserve a reception hall at an inn a few minutes out of town. But Adam and Leigh's guests wanted to congratulate them and wish them well now. One after the other they came through a receiving line.

Finally Jared was standing before them. Shawna and Danielle had already given them hugs, and Chad had shaken their hands.

Jared smiled at them now and said to Leigh, ''I hope someday my daughter finds a man as good as Adam.'' Then he looked at his son. ''I hope Mark and Chad each find a woman as lovely and compassionate as Leigh. I don't want you two to be strangers, you hear? In fact, we might have to set up once-a-month family gatherings, just to make sure everybody keeps in touch.''

''We'll probably be there more than you want us,'' Adam joked. ''Especially after Mark comes home.'' They were all praying for that day, and Adam was beginning to believe it would happen.

''Even when you get busy with building your camp?''

''Even then,'' Adam assured him.

''I won't tie you up any longer. I know you want

to get to the reception.'' He gave Leigh a hug, and then he gave Adam one, too.

When Jared moved away, Lissa and Sullivan took his place. Lissa hugged Leigh, and then with an uncertain smile, she tightly hugged Adam. He squeezed her back, wanting to know so much more about his twin. She and Sullivan had come to dinner one night this week so he and Leigh could tell them about their plans and personally invite them to the wedding. He had a feeling the four of them were going to be good friends.

Lissa leaned away from him, and her smile was so bright, he knew she was thoroughly happy for him. ''When are you and Leigh coming to the vineyard?'' she asked now.

''We're flying to Hawaii for two weeks. We both want some consistent sun,'' he joked. ''When we come back, I promise I'll bring you a lei and deliver it personally.''

''I think I'm going to like having you for a brother!''

After Lissa and Sullivan moved away, he and Leigh were finally alone. Everyone else had gone ahead to the reception.

''Well, Mrs. Bartlett? How does it feel?''

''How does what feel?'' she asked coyly.

Wrapping his arm around her, he pulled her close. ''How does it feel to be married to me?''

Her teasing tone gone now, she looked up at him

with her big blue eyes and decided, ''It feels wonderful.''

That was all Adam needed to hear. In the silence of the barn chapel, with the scent of gardenias permeating the air around them, he kissed Leigh as a man kisses his wife. They were united forever...united in soul, heart and body.

And this was only the beginning.

* * * * *

Don't miss the next emotional
LOGAN'S LEGACY *book,*
AND THEN THERE WERE THREE,
by Lynda Sandoval,
in April 2004.

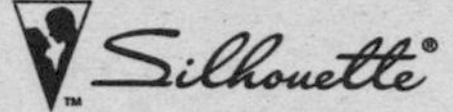

SPECIAL EDITION™

MERLYN COUNTY

Delivering the miracle of life...and love!

Meet the newest arrivals to
Merlyn County Regional Hospital, in

FOREVER...AGAIN

by Maureen Child

(Silhouette Special Edition #1604)

Widower Ron Bingham had married the love of his life, and he knew that when it came to true love, there was no such thing as second chances. But now, city girl Lily Cunningham's feisty flirtations and blond beauty had gotten under his skin—and into his soul—making him think maybe he could have forever...again.

On sale April 2004!

Don't miss the conclusion of Merlyn County Midwives!
IN THE ENEMY'S ARMS by Pamela Toth
(Silhouette Special Edition #1610, available May 2004)

Get your copy at your favorite retail outlet.

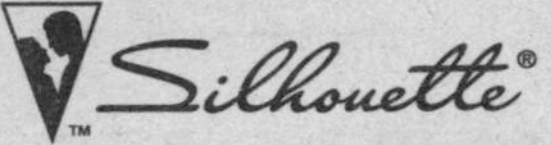

SPECIAL EDITION®

COMING NEXT MONTH

#1603 PRICELESS—Sherryl Woods
Million Dollar Destinies
Famed playboy Mack Carlton loved living the fast life—with even faster women—until he met Dr. Beth Browning. Beth's reserved, quiet ways brought out the deepest emotions in Mack, and soon had him wanting to believe in a slow and easy, forever kind of love. Could Mack convince Beth that his bachelor days were over?

#1604 FOREVER...AGAIN—Maureen Child
Merlyn County Midwives
You don't get a second chance at forever. That's what widower Ron Bingham believed. But, then, he hadn't counted on meeting PR whiz Lily Cunningham. The carefree beauty brought laughter and passion back into his life and made him wonder—was love even sweeter the second time around?

#1605 CATTLEMAN'S HEART—Lois Faye Dyer
Chaotic. That was the only way Rebecca Wallingford could describe her latest business trip. The superorganized accountant had been sent to oversee the expansion of a certain Jackson Rand's ranch. She'd never meant to get pulled into a whirlwind love affair with the rugged rancher...and she certainly hadn't planned on liking it!

#1606 THE SHEIK & THE PRINCESS IN WAITING—Susan Mallery
Prince Reyhan had been commanded by his father, the King of Bahania, to marry as befit his position. There was just one tiny matter in the way: divorcing his estranged wife, Emma Kennedy. Seeing sweet Emma again brought back a powerful attraction...and something deeper. Could Reyhan choose duty over his heart's desire?

#1607 THE BEST OF BOTH WORLDS—Elissa Ambrose
Single. Unemployed. Pregnant. Becky Roth had a lot on her mind...not to mention having to break her pregnancy news to the father, Carter Prescott III. They'd shared one amazing night of passion. But small-town, small-*time* Becky was no match for Carter's blue-blooded background. The fact that she was in love with him didn't change a thing.

#1608 IN HER HUSBAND'S IMAGE—Vivienne Wallington
Someone was trying to sabotage Rachel Hammond's ranch. The widowed single mom's brother-in-law, Zack Hammond, arrived and offered to help find the culprit...but the sexy, rugged photographer stirred up unwelcome memories of their scandalous past encounter. Now it was just a matter of time before a shattering secret was revealed!

SSECNM0304R